the
millennium
file

the millennium file

glenn anderson

Copyright © 1986
Horizon Publishers & Distributors, Inc.

All rights reserved. Reproduction in whole or any parts thereof in any form or by any media without written permission is prohibited.

ISBN: 0-88290-280-6
Library of Congress Catalog No.: 86-081774
Horizon Publishers Catalog & Order No.: 1966
First Printing, 1986

Printed and distributed
in the United States of America by

& Distributors, Incorporated
50 South 500 West   P.O. Box 490
Bountiful, Utah 84010-0490

Table of Contents

**Part One:
DREAMS OF MEN
9**

**Part Two:
WHISPERS FROM THE DUST
61**

**Part Three:
THE FINAL STANDOFF
101**

I
Dreams of Men

They shuffled along the dim passageway, a parade of trunkless, two-legged elephants with beetle eyes. Steam curled around their heads, trailing in the cold. A single, tipped antenna sprouted from behind the left eye of each of the creatures, where a rumple of gray creases took the place of an ear. One by one they crunched over shards of ice, past the hot red glow of a half-dozen laserflares anchored along the walls of the tunnel. Rounding a final bend the beasts headed up and out, through the mouth of the cave and into the howling Arctic dusk. One of the creatures, the last in line, hung back reluctantly. It pushed the bulging snow shields to its forehead, and from beneath the insect eyes squinted those of a human being.

Lee McKesson, clothed in a Thermofoam snow suit, stared back down the corridor. It was bathed in red, still clouded with the haze of the passing archaeologists' breath. To an outside observer it might have looked like a frozen version of Dante's Inferno. But to Lee, after nearly eight months of painstaking excavation, it was simply "the digs." Almost homey, she thought, in a wierd sort of way. It was her first research expedition, and despite the cold and the isolation and the incredibly long hours, she had found herself enjoying it.

"Miss McKesson, we're on the pad. I would suggest that you join us." Hoeksberg's voice quacked impatiently through the antenna and into Lee's left ear. She sighed.

Except for Hoeksberg, she was enjoying it.

"Dr. Roth's not up yet," she answered, and abruptly, for no particular reason, she felt a dark wave of uneasiness. "I thought I might stay behind and give him a hand . . ."

"Roth's never up on time, and I don't intend to allow you to join him in his total disregard for the rules of the Institute. Report immediately." The voice was not harsh, just coldly authoritarian. Lee set her jaw.

"Yes, sir."

She popped the shields back down over her eyes and headed up toward the digiport pad. Hoeksberg was a pain. Lee knew all along that he would be. She had talked to a lot of his graduates, and not one had delivered a glowing report. Even so, she had decided to apply for an assistantship under his direction. Because Hoeksberg had clout, and clout meant money, and money meant decent projects. In fact, if it hadn't been for her affiliation with Hoeksberg, she would probably be back at the university right now grading somebody's students' forty-page term papers. Or doing something else almost as fascinating.

Lee plodded the last few steps to the mouth of the cavern, tugging at the seat of her Thermofoams. She hated foams. They were warm, sure, but they itched like crazy. And they bagged all over the place, which always made her feel like a walking accumulation of double chins. Outside, twenty yards away, the rest of the party huddled, waiting on the digiport pad. Snow eddied in the arc lights.

Lee glanced back over her shoulder just once more knowing full well that Dr. Roth would not be there. She felt that gnawing apprehension again, like something cold settling half-way between her throat and her stomach.

Something was wrong with Roth.

She couldn't quite put her finger on it, but she could feel it. He hadn't really been himself for days. This morning had been worse than ever. Even if the others hadn't seemed to notice, Lee had. Since they were the only two

Mormons on the expedition, she and Roth had spent a lot of time together. They had shared conversation over meals for the first few months. Then Lee had begun dropping down to the digiport bay in the evenings to chat with Roth as he sorted artifacts and scanned specimens. Eventually she had come to know as much about his research project as she did about her own. Now as she stood and looked back into the empty maw of the ice cave, worry throbbing in her chest, Lee suddenly realized how much she had come to care for him. What if something were to happen down there, with the storm picking up and everyone else gone..?

"Miss McKesson, we're *waiting*!" Hoeksberg's voice had taken a harsher turn. Lee pushed the dread away as best she could and picked up her pace. Kicking up short poofs of snow, she poofed her way to the pad, avoided Hoeksberg's gaze and took her place among the others. Only moments later the researchers were gone, their bodies translated into a focused beam of energy and drawn back to their base camp some thirty-five miles away. All that remained was the furious wind, a steadily increasing snowfall, and Roth.

2

About a half-mile in from the opening to the caves, at the far edge of excavation site five, Dr. Derek Roth hunkered down. He chiseled carefully at the frozen earth, a humming laserflare held overhead. Next to him an air tractor bobbed slowly, almost imperceptibly, scarcely six inches off the ground. It was loaded nearly to overflowing with an assortment of pots and other earthen vessels, a heap of clay fragments, and a smattering of stones. Each was imbedded with a microscopic collection of organic matter which was Roth's stock-in-trade. Because, unlike most of his colleagues, Dr. Roth's specialty was not archeology per se, but zoology. Sometimes that alienated him a little from the rest of the team, but so be it. He had his own job to do, and he enjoyed it. It usually kept him out of Hoeksberg's path too, which was an added bonus.

And speaking of bonuses, he had just stumbled onto a whopper—something infinitely more exciting than the heap of samples on the tractor. He had been squatting before it for the last ten minutes, chipping it meticulously from the permafrost, ignoring the absence of the other researchers and the danger of the approaching storm.

He had found a human bone.

He flipped the chromium rock hammer around in his hand and ground at some of the finer earth with a clump of alloy bristles mounted in the handle. And as he flicked the grindings away with a careful finger, a feeling rippled through his head. It was a feeling he knew well.

He stopped cold, his steamy breath cut off in mid-puff. It's happening to me again, he thought. He lowered the flare, touching the ground with his fist to brace himself just in case.

But nothing happened. And now the feeling was gone, leaving him wondering if there really *had* been any feeling this time. After a moment's pause, he decided with a strange mixture of relief and disappointment that there hadn't been. He scratched his nose, like he always did when he was a little nervous, and set back to work on the bone.

At any other archeological site, a bone would have been the last thing to beamgram home about and Roth knew it. But here at the Nordaustlandet Corridors, things were different. There were bones, yes. Fish mostly, intermixed with scattered seal and caribou. But there were no human bones. There was not, in fact, the slightest trace of human remains. Impossible by professional consensus, but true nonetheless.

Today, though, that truth was going up for re-examination. Because Roth had something. It was flat and porous, yellowed to a deep amber by the perpetual damp. A shoulder blade perhaps? Yes, or a shard of pelvis. It was certainly nothing like any of the other animal specimens Roth had encountered over the past eight months. Not the right shape for a seal or a walrus and too small for a caribou. He held the laserflare down close, warming the frozen soil-and-gravel mixture that held the bone fast. He picked more quickly now, growing aware of the time he was taking, and eyed the specimen closely in the bright red light. Suddenly his heart sank.

The base of a large tooth appeared abruptly at the bottom edge of the piece. Roth felt at once let down and supremely foolish. It was just a chunk of jawbone, probably of a small whale, broken in just the right places to make it extremely deceptive. Nothing more. Roth rose to his feet. He silently chastised himself for his premature excitement, simultaneously breathing a sigh of relief that none of his co-workers had been within calling range.

And then, all at once, the feeling was back again.

It drifted clear through him, a light, detached sensation, as if the ground had suddenly washed out from under his feet. Roth felt his grip slacken on the laserflare. It slipped from his fingers and landed at his feet with a stuttery buzz, like a bumblebee glutted with pollen. Then the feeling hit him full force, harder than it had ever hit him before. Roth dropped to one knee, clinging to his last shred of consciousness, groping for the ground to steady himself. Then his arms buckled. He collapsed into the padding of his Thermofoams, limp and still.

But inside his head the pictures already whirled madly, rising like an ocean swell.

3

Scandinavia's ragged coasts hunched their shoulders against the wind. In a thousand-mile spiral, a sweeping mass of frigid air rolled out of the Arctic Circle and tore down the Barents Strait. To the south, it blasted inland toward the heart of Norway. To the north, across the strait, it battered the tiny Svalbard archipelago. On Nordaustlandet, the easternmost island in the group, a cluster of tiny lights bunched together in the gathering darkness. A half-dozen of them shone from the windows of Hoeksberg's research compound.

Lee stood inside, waiting beside one of the doors. She was a tall girl, pleasingly slender without the Thermofoam padding. Her auburn hair was clipped functionally short. Her face was lean, lightly freckled. But her brown eyes were deep and womanly. She stared grimly into a tiny video monitor, inset as part of a compact control panel to the left of the doorway. The monitor displayed a wide-angle view of the landscape outside. There, glacier fields stretched white and bare toward the North Atlantic where endless legions of dark-bottomed cumulo-stratus marched in on the gales of the storm. Snow blew freely now. Lee checked her watch, a paper-thin chromium band ticking off LCD microseconds. It had been nearly forty-five minutes, and still no sign of Roth.

"Sit down, would you McKesson? You're making me nervous." The voice came from Murray Hale, seated behind Lee in what they all loosely referred to as "the lounge." Murray was dark, hairy and muscular, a throwback to the days of gridirons and jock-itch. He always addressed Lee as "McKesson," in apparent disregard for her femininity. It was the only thing Lee even remotely liked about him. Right now, he was leaning over a scarred aluminum table reading an old Sports Illustrated. On the cover was a shot of an electropulse jai alai player, caught in mid-return with a plasmaball blazing in his racket.

"Sorry," Lee said emotionlessly, brushing him off like a burr from her sock. Her eyes were still riveted on the storm clouds. She reached for the digital temperature indicator just below the video monitor and punched three keys. A readout flashed onto the display. Twenty-two below. She punched three more for wind-chill factor.

Sixty-eight below.

Two more degrees and the electronics in the digiport pad would start freezing up. Roth would be stranded. Perhaps for hours, perhaps for days, depending upon the duration of the storm. Two years ago it had happened to a transfer student by the name of Shen Bergensen from Helsinki University. The storm had raged for three weeks without respite, rendering the Corridors totally inaccessible. When the weather finally cleared they had found Bergensen's body, frozen solid, jutting from a snowpack a mile and a half this side of the digs.

Lee sighed loudly and put a hand to the back of her neck, rotating her head to work out a crick. Daynia Wong glanced up from a long table at the back of the room, where she sat with three graduate students recording technical data from a mound of artifacts. Dr. Wong was old, but like most orientals, she didn't show it. The corners of her eyes crinkled with mild concern.

"Something wrong, Lee?" she asked.

Lee turned, wondering how much worry showed on her face. "Don't know," she said. " Maybe." But she *did* know. Roth had been late before but never this late. "Dr. Roth's still at the site. Wind-chill's at sixty eight. Could be a problem." She tried to shrug casually. Then she caught her lip starting to tremble and closed her mouth hard.

Murray snorted. "What are you, his nanny?"

Before Lee had the chance to respond with something decidedly un-Christian, Dr. Wong spoke. She was like a nodding Buddha, her eyes pinched off to nothing, her face relaxed into an imperishable smile.

"Dr. Roth is always late, is he not?" she asked. "As always, he will be along." With that she went back to work.

Lee just stared, momentarily furious at Wong's lack of concern. Then her anger ebbed. After all, ordinarily Wong would have been right. Roth *was* always late. Yet it rarely represented a problem, because he was always on top of things too. Lost in his work, yes—totally absorbed with some scrap of hide or fragment of plant fiber—but with an underlying presence of mind that never seemed to fail him. Lee knew that, as a rule, Roth would be well aware of the temperature outside the caves, usually to within a few degrees. He would know exactly how many minutes he would need to reach the pad, to dial in his coordinates and digiport himself back to the compound before the electronics began shutting down. Roth would know *all* of those things, and he would act accordingly.

As a rule.

But now? Lee didn't know. Because lately he had seemed . . . distracted. It was more than that though, she was sure. Lee was close to Roth, closer than anyone else in the research party. She had felt drawn to him almost immediately . . . before she had ever spotted the Standard Works sandwiched between genetics and computer science on his bookshelf. She had liked him from the very beginning—his drive, his genius, his boundless enthusiasm—and had admired him just as quickly. And, for some unknown but supremely gratifying reason, Lee detected that Roth felt much the same way about her. As the months passed, their affinity had deepened. Now Lee could honestly say that she knew Roth as well as she had ever known anyone. And she knew something wasn't right.

She kept thinking back to that morning. She had never been frightened like that before.

They had been sitting in the back of the lounge, eating breakfast. Roth was buttering a slice of protein loaf ("syn-toast", he called it) and smiling with thoughtful amusement. He was almost old enough to be Lee's father, but not quite. His face had the weather-worn look of a mountain climber, creased with the kind of wrinkles that suggested easy laughter. He took a bite of syn-toast and brushed his salt-and-pepper hair out of his eyes. Lee couldn't remember liking salt-and-pepper hair before meeting Roth. Now she found it quite attractive.

"What do *you* think it means?" he grinned.

The scriptures were open to Deuteronomy next to her plate. She swallowed a bite and scanned the column for the passage in question. They had run across it during one of their late-night scripture-study-and-shoot-the-Gospel-breeze sessions the previous evening. They had brushed over it without comment then. But the words had come back to her while she had been dressing that morning.

"Well, obviously it refers to the Lost Tribes, don't you think?"

He nodded with the same grin. "I think so, yes."

She stopped her finger at verse four. "So here's what it says: ' If any of thine be driven out unto the outmost parts of heaven, from thence will the Lord thy God gather thee, and from thence will he fetch thee'." She looked up at him. He raised his eyebrows.

"Just like the Enquirer article, huh Sis?" He usually called her that. It had evolved from 'Sister McKesson', a tongue-in-cheek nickname that was too long to stick in original form.

She winced and grinned back. The Enquirer article was a sore point with Hoeksberg. It was seldom mentioned above a whisper. "No. *Not* like the Enquirer article. But there are people who seem to think the tribes were zapped out into space or something. Maybe this scripture is where they got the idea in the first place. I just wondered what you think it means." Her eyes narrowed, feigning outrage at the expression on his face. "And stop giving me that smirk, unless you'd like a cup of reconstituted grapefruit juice all over it."

He laughed. His laugh always warmed her. "I think the passage simply means that the Lord is very determined to gather the tribes. And that he has more than enough power to do the job, no matter how difficult it might seem." He motioned at her with his fork. "But you're right, the choice of words there is interesting." She smiled, nodding in agreement. At that point she looked down at her plate and cut into a slice of syn-bacon so she could combine it with a bite of syn-eggs, silently wishing that the university supply master would repent of his syns and digiport them some real, honest-to-goodness food. Then she closed her scriptures and looked up again.

"It really is. I had a roommate once th . . . "

Her voice trailed off. Roth was sitting, fork in hand, with a lump of food suspended motionless over his plate. He was staring in Lee's direction, but he wasn't really looking at her. It was almost as if he were looking *through* her. His eyes were glassy, blind.

Lee stared at him for a long second. "Dr. Roth? . . . " she asked finally.

The fork slipped gently from his fingers and dropped like the free end of a seesaw—*plink*—onto his plate.

Alarm rose in her chest. "Dr. Roth," she repeated, "are you all right?" She glanced around the room. Everybody else was either gabbing or reading or clearing up to head out for the day. Not an eye was turned her way. She turned back, fully expecting to see Roth slump to the floor. This time he was staring right into her eyes. She started.

"What? . . . " he asked her dully, and blinked.

"I said, are you feeling okay?" Her voice was just a little shaky. She let a shudder escape along her arms. "You looked . . . " and she couldn't finish, because she couldn't decide exactly how he looked.

He stared at his plate and set his fork down deliberately. Then he took a deep breath. "I'm fine" he said, "just thinking." Then he had smiled easily, and they had started talking again. That was that. Obviously nothing to worry about.

Except that she had seen that same look before. It had come upon him several times over the last few weeks: a kind of dull detachment, a fleeting glassiness in his eyes. Like a mini-blackout, it came and then fled in the blink of an eye. But it had never been like this. This was more than just a lapse of concentration. This was spooky.

Yet how could she tell the others that? The words were on the tip of her tongue right now, and they just clung there, feeling incredibly silly. What was she going to say? That she was concerned because Roth let his mind wander while she was talking to him at breakfast? That she was worried because of the look in his eyes? *That's right, Dr. Wong. Every once in a while he just sort of drifts out. Plink goes the fork and it's zombie time. Or haven't you noticed? Well, maybe you should, because there's something wrong with him, and it scares the living daylights out of me. It looks just like . . .*

Suddenly she knew what it looked like. She remembered playing with her cousin Kerry, a borderline epileptic, who would just up and phase out whenever she forgot to take her regular medication.

Roth looked like that. He looked like he was having a seizure.

All at once Lee was on her way—stepping briskly, almost running—to one of the smaller departure bays adjoining the lounge. She moved inside, hurled open a storage cabinet and yanked out a set of Thermofoams. At the same time, Dr. Wong called in from across the room. Her voice had lost just a little of its composure.

"Lee..?"

"I'm going out after him," she called back. Her legs had already filled out some of the gray wrinkles, and she was pulling the suit over her shoulders.

Murray stared after her, his mouth half-open. If Lee had been in the right frame of mind she might have been amused. That kind of look rarely crossed his face.

"The kid's lost it," Murray said.

A split second later, Dr. Wong appeared at the door to the bay. "Lee," she said, " the rules . . . "

Lee just shook her head, jamming the snow shields down over her eyes and securing the flap across the lower half of her face. Back in the lounge, Wong's graduate students were gravitating away from their tables to see what all the ruckus was about. Murray gave an incredulous laugh that just barely penetrated the foam wrapping Lee's ears.

"You're crazy, McKesson. Hoeksberg's gonna fry your b . . . "

A loud warbling note cut him off. It was a digiport alert, prohibiting departure due to an incoming beam on the main bay. Wong turned to Lee, raised her eyebrows and smiled.

Roth was back.

4

Lee burst into the bay just as the lights on the digiport console had risen to full intensity, triggered by Roth's remote. The room was expansive and barren, its high ceiling and bare girders reminiscent of an old-fashioned warehouse. A few yards inside sat a sprawling jumble of equipment. The gear looked like it had dropped there on it's own, wires trailing helter-skelter. Barely a quarter of the electronics belonged to the digiporter; all the rest were of Roth's design, used in his research. Nothing cosmetic to be sure: all totally functional.

At the center of the room was the compound's main digiport pad, a silvery circle nearly twenty feet in diameter. The pad was military surplus, and the outer edge was frayed in places, lifting from the floor. The top surface was pockmarked with an infinite array of what looked like pinholes. Where the coating wasn't scuffed it still made little rainbows when the light reflected just right. The compound's largest pad, it was capable of transporting a total payload of nearly a hundred persons, or equipment or other material of comparable mass. Now, at the center, a small shaft of light began to grow as if pulled from the air. The light danced for just a second as the microchips took hold, placing it on the right coordinates. Then the pad issued a rushing buzz, like some enormous insect exhaling widemouthed, and the light flared to blinding intensity. Just as quickly the luminance was gone, and Roth stood there with his loaded air tractor, their atoms reassembled, looking somehow very small and insignificant after all the fireworks. He raised his snow shields and blinked a couple of times—a person's most common first reaction after digiportation—and smiled calmly at Lee.

"How goes it, Sis?"

She was still panting, eyeing him uncertainly. He was almost too casual. Or was it just her imagination? "Is everything okay?" she asked. The question came out with less urgency than she had expected.

"Shouldn't it be?" he asked.

Still smiling he stepped forward gingerly, mashing a button on his remote control to bring the air tractor along like an obedient dog. He pulled off his snow shields.

"You were out a long time," Lee returned. "We started to get a little worried." That was a fib, but just a small one: an *I* to a *we*. "You have any trouble?"

He hopped off the pad. "The only trouble I've got is too much to do and not enough time to do it in. Wanna set up the scan on these for me tonight?"

She nodded and smiled—but only a half-smile—as he gave the tractor an electronic shove through the air and parked it in a corner.

"Sure."

"Sis, you're terrific," he said, grinning openly. He yanked his foams open at the chest on his way to the door. "Give me a chance to get outta these and into a warm cup and I'll be right back. You want anything to drink?"

She shook her head and he did a double take, glancing back at her.

"Have a tough day? You look a little wrung out."

The question forced her to relax a little. "No . . . no, I'm fine," she returned. "Go get something to warm you up and I'll start laying these out." She motioned to the artifacts. There was still a lot on her mind, but the words on the tip of her tongue felt unavoidably silly again, so she kept them back. Perhaps another time, but not now.

Roth nodded, winked and charged through the door with characteristic zest.

* * *

But by the time he had hung up his foams in the small bay by the lounge, his smile had drifted into solemn reflection. He clicked the storage locker shut and stared at his hand. It was trembling.

Everything okay? He honestly couldn't say. At any rate, there was a whole world of things he wasn't telling Lee. Because he couldn't. Not yet. Not until he had figured them out for himself.

He lingered in the bay for awhile, pondering. After several minutes, the trembling stopped.

5

Lee sat in the darkened digiport bay facing a glowing yellow computer terminal. Positioned near-center to Roth's bank of equipment, the screen itself was about two feet across, a scant inch thick, and light enough to be anchored upright by a pair of small aluminum L bars. A black circular cursor blinked at Lee from the upper left corner. A timeworn keyboard rested in front of the screen, mute evidence to the ongoing academic struggle for financial support. In industry, virtually all computers were now voice activated. Top-of-the-line defense models were linked via bioprobes to their operators, who controlled the machines with thought waves and nerve impulses. But collegiate researchers had to settle for what they could afford, and Roth was stuck with a keyboard. Lee shrugged. It was better than nothing.

Her fingers set to work on the keys and the cursor skittered to the left, trailing a line of crisp, black characters about a half-inch tall: Lee's full name, the date and time, the project and excavation site numbers. As she clicked off the information, Roth stepped from the darkness into the yellow glow behind her, a cup of cocoa steaming in his hand.

"Logged on already?" he asked, and slurped at his overly hot chocolate.

She nodded. "Just finished." As she completed the last digit of the site number, the screen suddenly went blank. There was a low, double beep, and the cursor spit across the screen to the upper left corner, waiting. She paused for just a second.

"The code . . . ?" Roth started to ask.

"I know it, I know it," she cut in with good-natured impatience. "I'll remember it. Just hang on." She thought for a second and couldn't help smiling. Despite the fact that Roth had none of the trappings of an ambitious entrepreneur, he was certainly no dummy. This was the third and most sophisticated of his gene-scan programs, and he had protected every one with a complicated access code to lock out unauthorized users. It wasn't as if Nordaustlandet were swarming with computer pirates. But after all, the program was one of a kind, and it would only be a matter of time before it was commercialized.

Her fingers tapped across the keys, ticking off one line of digits and then another. It had taken her a while to become this conversant with the system, and her masters project had suffered for it. She knew that, but she let it suffer. Roth's research utterly fascinated her. Perhaps she would be changing programs soon anyway. A change of advisors right about now wouldn't hurt her outlook on life, either.

Her fingers stopped abruptly in mid-air.

"Is it a two-one or a one-two at the end of the third series?" she asked. She squinted, trying to recall.

"I thought you said you'd remember it," he chided.

"I do," she snapped triumphantly, and typed it in:

The screen went blank. There was a low double beep, and the cursor spit across to the upper left corner again. Lee groaned, and Roth chuckled through his nose as he swallowed another sip.

"One-two," he corrected.

She stuck her tongue out at him and he chuckled once again as she started typing it over. Actually, in spite of the complicated hard and software involved, the concept behind gene-scanning was relatively easy to understand. The computer input was tied to a compact, cylindrical robot— the "scannerbot," Roth called it. The scannerbot possessed a single, telescoping arm. On the end of that arm was a minute genetic sensing device called a "scan head." During a gene scan, the scannerbot would pass the head over the surface of selected artifacts, automatically searching out any fragments of organic material. Usually the fragments consisted of microscopic particles—plant or animal tissue—either clinging to or imbedded in the porous clay. The scan head was sensitive enough to detect particles as small as a single cell, and whenever it found anything, it probed for genetic make-up. The program automatically ignored any samples detected previously. But it sent all unrecognized genetic information to the computer in the form of electronic data. That data would, in turn, appear on the screen.

The process was ingenious, but it was only the beginning.

Because Roth had tied the computer *output* into the digiport pad. So, once he had the data on the screen, he could multiply it electronically to represent the entire organism. Then, with the touch of a button, he could translate the data into light energy, shoot it out onto the pad, and viola! The electronic "clone" would reassemble itself into something quite tangible—anything from a stalk of marsh grass to a fur seal.

Or a woolly mammoth.

Of course, the woolly mammoth incident was not the most pleasant to dwell on, so Lee pushed it out of her mind and kept on typing.

"There," she said with a breath of finality, and entered the completed code. Roth nodded, grunting with approval.

"Not bad, Sis. Not bad at all. You made the grid tracing already?"

"While you were taking your time in the lounge," she returned. "Take a look."

They both watched. Whipping from left to right, the cursor drew a grid across the terminal. It corresponded square for square to a larger metal grid spread across the floor at the far side of the bay. Then the cursor began again, this time leaving a set of irregular outlines arranged precisely over the squares. The outlines were artifacts.

Lee glanced out across the room. The grid was there, about eight feet square, stretched out under a single spotlight. On the grid, spaced evenly, was about half of all the stuff Roth had brought back from the digs in the air tractor. Lee hadn't been able to fit everything on, but what was there now showed up as the irregular shapes on the computer screen. While Roth had been getting his cocoa, she had carefully traced the widest surfaces of all the artifacts with the tip of the robot arm. Now, once set in motion, the scannerbot would work all night by itself, moving systematically over the grid and working the scan head over every square inch of each stone and pottery fragment. If it found anything, the data would be waiting for Roth in the computer the next morning.

He whistled with admiration. "Okay," he nodded, "let's scan it." Lee pressed a series of keys and the scannerbot whirred to life.

Actually, Roth's scanning process was just one in a long series of steps undertaken to recreate the ancient environment of the Corridors. Through his work, Roth had been able to gather a wealth of information about the plants and animals used by the caves' ancient inhabitants—for food, clothing, tools—what have you. Ordinarily, he could have used the same process to scan for remains of the inhabitants themselves. But here at Nordaustlandet that was impossible, because there were no human remains.

That, of course, was unbelievable. But unbelievable or not, it was undeniably true.

To date, some eighty-five gene scans had come up empty-handed. Roth had not found so much as a human hair, or a fingernail fragment in a burial jar. Not one, single, solitary cell. Zilch. The whole thing was easily remarkable enough to have been publicized as one of the century's most baffling enigmas, if Hoeksberg hadn't played it down so much to avoid sensationalist media coverage. The truth of the matter, Lee supposed, was that Hoeksberg judged the situation to be just as sensational as everyone else did. He just wasn't saying anything.

Neither was Lee, but she knew what she thought. She and Roth had batted it around on several occasions.

In approximately 720 B.C., during the seventh year of the reign of Hoshea, king of Israel, the Assyrians overran Samaria. Then they swarmed into northern Israel to complete their conquest. In the process they captured ten of Israel's twelve tribes and carried them away slaves toward the north. And there, recorded history made an end of the subject. Although the scriptures foretold that they would one day return from the lands of the North, no one really had any idea where the Lost Ten Tribes had ended up.

Lee had an inkling. She felt certain that at least some of them had ended up in the caves at Nordaustlandet. There was no solid evidence of that fact as yet, except perhaps for some pottery that exhibited certain characteristics that *might* be interpreted as Assyrian. And others that *might* be interpreted as Hebrew. Nevertheless, how else could you explain the fact that every trace of the Corridors' ancient inhabitants had disappeared? In Lee's mind there was only one explanation. They were removed and tucked away somewhere by divine intervention.

Roth was pretty noncommittal about the whole idea, although she knew that he didn't wholly dismiss it. However, neither one of them would have dared vocalize it within earshot of Hoeksberg, especially after the International Enquirer Article.

NEW EVIDENCE: LOST TRIBES OF ISRAEL KIDNAPPED BY ALIENS!

Hoeksberg was outraged by the headline. The article itself was even worse. It provided conclusive proof that the ancient cave dwellers at Nordaustlandet—revealed as the Lost Tribes—had been abducted en masse by a band of extraterrestrials. The theory was corroborated by the magazine's official board of psychics. Of course, the story did nothing for Hoeksberg's professional image, let alone that of the project. He screamed, wrote letters, demanded retractions, threatened lawsuits. Finally, the publicity just died out on its own.

Once that happened, everyone settled down to business again. And it was uncanny how quickly they all got used to the idea that *homo sapiens* remains were just not to be found. There simply were no human bones, and there simply were not *going* to be any human bones. It was an anomaly, but the researchers had no choice but to shrug it off. As was the case with most enigmas, the answer, no doubt, would eventually come.

Privately, Lee wondered.

She listened to the scannerbot whine, watching the cursor blink over the outlines on the screen as it followed the path of the scan head.

"You're really getting the hang of this, Sis," Roth said, beaming without restraint. She looked over at him. The glow from the screen highlighted the ruggedness of his jaw line. His eyes gleamed youthfully, crinkled at the corners with smile-wrinkles. Lee felt a sudden rush of tenderness. It was so good to have Roth back. And all at once she longed to tell him so, to draw closer, to touch his cheek and brush the hair back from his eyes, to tell him how much it meant to have him safe and hear his voice and feel his smile. Almost unconsciously, she slid a half-step in his direction.

Then the door to the bay opened. Lee glanced over quickly, her heart pulsing, and slid a half-step back again. The silhouette there was unmistakable, if only because of its authoritarian stance. It was Hoeksberg.

"Good evening," he said, without warmth. "Miss McKesson, you will have to excuse Mr. Roth and myself. We must talk." Hoeksberg stood still by the door, holding it open. The invitation to leave was characteristically blunt. Roth stared at him, then gave her a soft nod.

"See you in the morning. If I'm not in by six you can start running the cloning series yourself, huh? "

She nodded back. Roth's eyes reflected composure, but that was typical even in the face of trouble, which she supposed this was.

"Sure," she said simply, and headed out the door. He smiled after her.

"Good work."

She gave him a quick smile in return, then brushed past Hoeksberg with a respectful glance.

* * *

He didn't look at Lee. He just closed the door behind her and stood looking at Roth, who finally stepped to a nearby console and brought up what lights there were in the room. He took another sip of his cocoa, which by now was growing quite cold, plopped down in one tattered chair and gestured to another.

"Sit down, Roald," Roth said. "It's been a long day."

Hoeksberg eyed him for a moment more before responding to the invitation. Roth gazed back pleasantly, refusing to betray the slightest tension.

"You were late again this evening," Hoeksberg said. "Dangerously late."

Roth broke his gaze for another slug of cold cocoa. "Mmmm," he nodded, drinking. "I found some samples at site five. Took me a while to load them up."

"Mr. Roth," Hoeksberg said quietly, "over the past several months you have shown an open contempt for the regulations of the International Geographic Institute, a major source of funding for this project. You have never ceased to strain those regulations. On many occasions you have broken them outright, as you did this evening." His face was cold and hard, chiseled out of deep shadow. "I would like to hear a response to your behavior."

Roth looked at him for a moment and finally shrugged. "You're right," he said, because there was simply nothing else to say. But the words sounded more insubordinate than he had intended. Hoeksberg eyed him silently, perhaps at least a little nonplussed.

"Roald," Roth began, "you and I both know that those regulations were drawn up by a bunch of bottom-heavy bureaucrats to protect their own tails from legal recourse. That's all. They live in an ivory tower and half of them have never even gotten their hands dirty, let alone worked on a dig. They can write all the rules they want, but when you're out on the job, sometimes you just have to run on instincts and *they* don't always operate according to the rules. They just don't. When you're on the firing line, you do what needs to be done, whether section twelve, subparagraph B says you're supposed to do it or not. That's how breakthroughs are made, not by keeping one eye on the digs and the other one in the rule book. You know that as well as I do."

Hoeksberg heard him out emotionlessly. "Mr. Roth," he said finally, "you are endangering my project."

Roth let out a disgusted breath. He hadn't really expected Hoeksberg to buy his little speech, but he had wanted to get it off his chest for a long time anyway. He started to speak again, and Hoeksberg cut him off abruptly.

"You arrived at the compound over an hour late. You were within two degrees of possible entrapment at the site. And if you had indeed become trapped, you might very well have been responsible for risking another life as well."

Roth squinted at him. "What are you talking about? . . . "

"Miss McKesson," Hoeksberg continued, "was in the east departure bay preparing to return to the digs when you digiported in. Her intent, I suppose, was to rescue you."

Roth let out a heavy breath. But underneath there was a trace of a smile he couldn't hold back. Sis was really something. Thank goodness he had arrived back at the compound in time.

"Mr. Roth, I needn't remind you that you are here at Dr. Foley's behest, not mine. I granted the zoology department a personal favor in allowing your participation here."

Roth snorted under his breath. Personal favor. That was a laugh. Hoeksberg had never granted a personal favor in his life. The truth of the matter was, Foley's father-in-law had just received an appointment to the trustee's office, and Hoeksberg was playing politics. He already had connections sewn up with the rest of the trustees.

"Your contribution to this project has been marginal at best," Hoeksberg continued. "It is certainly no compensation for your glaring insufficiencies. I am through tolerating them. From this point forward you will respect the rules of the Institute, as do the other members of our team. Or you will cease to be a affiliated with it."

Roth sat relaxed, unmoved. Things were bound to have come to this sooner or later. He and Hoeksberg had been bumping heads lightly for months. Now it was time for a major skull fracture. And, unfortunately, Hoeksberg did not make idle threats.

Roth smiled and scratched his nose.

"I have no intention of allowing you to place the standing of this project in jeopardy," Hoeksberg concluded, his voice quiet but deadly. "Do you understand?"

"Of course," Roth stated calmly.

He sat back as Hoeksberg excused himself and stepped into the darkness. Roth listened to the door close behind him. Then he breathed a long, tense sigh. For several minutes, Roth sat reflecting in silence. He thought about his career, about his project, about what had happened earlier that evening, back at the cave.

Something was back there, waiting for him.

Roth looked down at his hands. They were trembling again.

6

The night continued, bitter and moonless. The snow stopped falling at approximately 2:00 A.M., but the wind screamed on, driving drifts before it like scudding waves in the darkness. It raced and howled, pulling the remnants of the storm clouds from the sky and whipping them through glacial valleys as currents of mist.

Roth lay in his bed at the south end of the compound, dreaming. In the dream, he was standing in what looked like the digiport bay, except that it was now missing its walls and ceiling. All of the digiport and scanning gear, precisely arranged, was simply perched on the open crest of a moonlit hill. The air was crisp but comfortable. Ground fog spread a thick quilt around the base of the equipment, lapping at the edge of the digiport pad. There, sitting cross-legged, caressed by fingers of vapor, sat an old man. He wore a rough-woven robe, concealed at the chest by a generous gray beard. He motioned Roth over.

"Come, Brother Derek," he invited, "and we shall talk." He patted a spot next to him on the pad. Fog puffed out from under his hand.

Roth stepped over. The old man smiled congenially. Up close, there was something oddly familiar about him. It took only a second for Roth to put his finger on it. The old man's face looked like a wizened version of an old 2-D movie star: Omar Sharif. Yet there was something else familiar about him as well. It was his voice. There was something about his voice.

He patted the pad again and Roth sat. The old man chuckled good-naturedly and put his arm around Roth's shoulder, squeezing it. He gave Roth a gentle slap on the back.

"How doest thou feel, Brother Derek?" he asked.

Roth gazed at him for a moment. Somehow the old man's eyes mirrored everything: Roth's project, his discussion with Hoeksberg, his experience in the cave. Everything.

"I feel scared," Roth said, suddenly willing to let it all out. His voice cracked. "I don't know what's been happening to me. I don't know why . . . "

His voice trailed off. There was no point in continuing. The old man already knew how Roth felt. That was in his eyes too. He gave Roth another squeeze.

"Fear not," he said. "Thou hast an errand from the Lord." He said it so matter-of-factly, as if it happened every day. Roth just nodded. He felt like a little boy sitting next to his grandpa. The old man's expression grew more serious.

"Remain faithful. Challenges await thee. And dangers. But He will guide thee, and protect thee. And He will call others to thy cause. Be patient and take heart. In time, thine eyes will be opened." He smiled and nodded. "Yes, in time."

Roth sat listening. He expected more, but there was none. The old man rose to his feet.

"But . . . why me?" Roth demanded. He stood, dwarfing the old man beside him, who chuckled again.

"Why?" he echoed. He swept his arm toward the equipment arranged under the stars. "Behold. What seest thou?"

Roth looked. The scannerbot was there, along with his trace grid and his incredible dinosaur of a computer system that sprawled in a half-dozen oversized components. His whole project was there.

"Electronic equipment," he shrugged. Obviously, that was not a particularly inspired answer. But it was all that he saw.

The old man nodded. "Yes," he beamed, "and all assembled as only thine hand could have done. With His guidance, to be sure. He has been leading thee from the very beginning. Did thou not know?"

Roth started to shake his head. Then he stopped short. Actually, when he thought about it that way, he *did* know. All at once it seemed quite obvious. The program, the robot, the scan head configuration, the digiport interface . . . how could he possibly have come up with all of that on his own?

"Seest thou?" the old man smiled. "And He will lead thee now as well. But make thou haste. Tonight, Brother Derek. Thou art called to begin *tonight*."

He turned and stepped toward the center of the pad. Roth spun to face him.

"But why? What is it all for..?"

"In time," the old man repeated, "your eyes will be opened." The light had already begun to dance, to kindle his form into glowing plasma. Roth's eyes widened with panic.

"No! Wait..!" he called, scrambling after him. "Just tell me *why*!" He reached for the rough-woven robe and his hand parted it like a ghost. The old man was already digiporting away, Roth's cries echoing after him in the night.

* * *

He awakened to darkness with his blanket crumpled in his hand. Outside, ice crystals machine-gunned the building in irregular volleys. Roth lay for an hour or more, unable to sleep. Off and on, he prayed. The wind shrieked back at him, threatening.

Finally all doubt was gone, and he knew. He was going to have to go back out to the digs. Somehow, for some reason, he had a task to perform. And he had to perform it tonight.

He had felt inklings of it coming on for some time. When had they first started? Nearly two weeks ago, perhaps a little longer. At first there was little more than a fleeting impression, like an idea out of nowhere, gone as quickly as it had come. The sensation came at odd times: while he was showering, on the way up to the pad from the caves, once during a post-breakfast conversation with Wong over the prospects for the university's upcoming athletic season. Sometimes, as time went on, he found the impression lingering in his mind, refusing to disappear, ebbing and flowing in his subconscious.

Then, before long, came the pictures. The images were intangible at first, hard to get a handle on and remember. But as they invaded his brain more frequently, more vividly, he could both see and recall them clearly. They were always the same.

They showed him an urn, framed in his head like a close-up in a video-hologram. The pot was ancient and water-stained, protruding from a dark mantle of permafrost. The lip of the vessel was ringed with metal, tarnished but still smooth, and at least one additional ring was also visible, imbedded in the vessel's neck. Roth had seen it clearly, probably a dozen times. The last few instances had been so striking that they had brought a physical sensation along with them—a dizzy, buoyant feeling, as if all of his weight were softly draining out into the air.

Up until early this evening, he hadn't the slightest idea what to make of it all.

At first he thought he was just succumbing to fatigue, allowing his mind to wander. Later he wondered if perhaps the image was something akin to the repeating dreams he sometimes had as a child. In one of the most memorable he had flown countless times, spread-eagle, over a prehistoric landscape, watching a herd of brontosaurus feed in a swamp. Perhaps, he had mused, this was the same kind of thing.

Now though, he had no doubts. The image was not a product of his own weary mind. It had come from Heaven.

He repeated the statement, calmly and logically in his mind. He knew how it sounded. If Hoeksberg or any of the others on the team knew what he was thinking they would presume he was losing touch. Phasing out. Tipping the gourd and losing all of the seeds, as they say. He might even have wondered himself, if it hadn't been for the dream.

And the voice. The voice cinched it.

He had finished unearthing that obnoxious jawbone and was rubbing the shin of his professional ego, which had just received a sharp kick. Turning away from his find with a snort of disgust, he had taken a step toward the air tractor. He knew he was late, that the wind was probably already coming up, licking the heat from the digiport pad like marrow from a bone. He had wasted a lot of time, and now he had to get back. Fast.

That was when it hit him again—that hazy, upended feeling that always brought on the close-up of the urn. But this time it kept on coming, swelling, bursting into his mind and overflowing into the rest of him like an injection of light from a giant hypodermic. And suddenly he was flying again, just like he used to over the prehistoric swamp. Only now he was flying through the caves, over site five and on past sites six and seven. Clear to site fourteen, the last that Hoeksberg had officially opened to this year's excavation. And he kept going.

Within a short time (at least it *seemed* short) the corridor branched in a clog of icy stalactites. Roth glided to the left, through the smaller of the two openings. The passageway flowed, weaved, narrowed, constricting almost to nothing. Then it suddenly opened again over a yawning pit. Roth swung into it and spiraled down, buzzing a throng of startled ice formations that twisted row after row of slick, rounded heads in his direction. Finally reaching the bottom, he slowed at the far side of the pit. Then he banked to the right and slipped through a narrow fissure into a massive adjoining chamber.

There, just inside and slightly to the left, was a dark mantle of permafrost. It jutted like a cartoon tongue from the toothy grin of a long row of stalactites and stalagmites.

Lodged there, close enough for Roth to have touched, was the urn.

At that moment, from somewhere distant, a voice said: "Derek, hurry. You must leave now."

And then the urn was gone, and Roth was opening his eyes, focusing slowly on the rocky ceiling above site five. He lay there on the ground for a moment, totally drained, listening to his heart, his breathing, the drone of the laser-flare he had dropped earlier as it flickered next to his head. The air tractor still bobbed patiently nearby.

Roth sat up, blinked and scratched his nose.

"Whoa," he now remembered saying softly. The recollection made him laugh out loud. It must have rated as the great-grandaddy of all understated exclamations. To Roth's surprise, his limbs all seemed to work just fine. He actually was *not* utterly exhausted, as he had first imagined when he had come to on the floor.

The voice came again, still and small, but piercingly clear. "Derek, hurry. You must leave. *Now*."

He rose immediately to his feet and shook himself out of the daze. Time felt suddenly alien to him, as if there really were no such concept, and he realized that he had no idea whatsoever of how long he had been lying there. He fished in his front trouser pouch for the remote control to the air tractor. A tiny, blinking chronometer was housed above the controls. He held it up to view and swallowed hard. He had been unconscious (or . . . whatever it was that he had been) for over half an hour. Outside, the mercury had been steadily falling the entire time.

He half ran, half-stumbled up to the mouth of the Corridors. It wasn't easy. Running panic-stricken in foams was a lot like trying to snap your fingers to a catchy tune with boxing gloves on. Anyway, when he had finally made it up to the thermoindicator on the pad and punched in the wind-chill, it had registered sixty-nine below. He made it back to the compound with one degree to spare.

Now he lay in the darkness, reliving the experience again and again, thinking about the urn, and the route that led to it through the Corridors, and the voice that had awakened him and quite possibly saved his life.

He knew now who that voice belonged to. It belonged to the old man in the dream.

Make thou haste. Tonight, Brother Derek . . .

There was no question about it. The urn was apparently the object of some divine purpose. How did Roth know? His certainty went beyond the dream and the voice. He had an errand from the Lord, and he *felt* it. And what was more, with a hint of urgency that both surprised and somehow excited him, Roth also felt that retrieving the urn was but the first step in that errand.

Retrieving the urn. That, certainly, was a task that could not be accomplished during any of the routine daily excavations. Hoeksberg had marked all of this year's sites clearly, and the rest of the caverns were off limits until they had been fully scouted. The urn was unmistakably out of bounds, and its resting place would probably not be scouted for a year or more.

Tonight, Brother Derek. Thou art called to begin tonight . . .

He turned under the covers. He had been lying in bed for nearly an hour fighting the notion off, but he just couldn't get out from under it.

He had to go after the urn. Tonight.

The prompting was inescapable. But *why?* Why risk the storm for some old clay jug that nobody'd given a second thought about for the last thousand-or-so years? How was he going to locate it, and what was he going to do with the urn once he got it? And what in heaven's name was he going to do if Hoeksberg found out?

All of his questions remained unanswered.

In time, thine eyes will be opened. In time...

Roth heaved a sigh and shook his head resolutely. Then he swept the covers back and swung his feet out onto the cold floor. No, the answers he sought tonight were not to be found in prayer. They lay imbedded in a mantle of permafrost, a good hour past the deepest explored reaches of the Nordaustlandet Corridors.

And that was where he was headed, totally unaware that before the night was over he would find himself in a desperate battle for his life.

7

The dark of the cave was dense and biting. Roth plucked a laserflare from the bundle in his left hand, extended it away from his face and squeezed the pressure switch in the handle. The tip erupted with a snap, revealing a fork in the tunnel. The passages diverged unevenly, separated by a glistening tangle of stalactites and icicles, opening much more widely to the right.

It was the same divergence he had seen in the... vision. That was what it was, he knew now. A vision.

Roth bore to the left, squeezing past the writhing ice formation and into a narrow, low-ceilinged crawlspace. The fit was claustrophobically tight. Wound over his right shoulder he carried a coil of rope. Strapped across his back was a flat metal pack about three inches thick with a fluted, double exhaust jutting from the underside. It was the compound's only jet pack. Roth was going to need it, he was sure, to get down into the pit.

He was now far away from the opening to the cave, from the furious howl of the wind. He had materialized on the pad at about 3:00, the temperature poised at an unsettling sixty-nine below. With luck it would hold steady throughout the night, until its expected dip just before sunrise. This time of year, that was typically about eleven-thirty in the morning. Of course, he would have to be back at the compound well before that, or there would be the devil to pay.

Roth edged along the passage, scrunching his foams through the narrowest spots like a fat man passing through a mass-transit turnstile. So far, his route through the cavern had been clearly recognizable . . . more so, in fact, than he ever would have imagined. Details jumped out at him, triggering recollections that were already firmly rooted in his mind. A formation here, an overhang there. It was as if he had covered this ground before—not just once in some sort of dreamflight, but many, many times—like an old haunt from his childhood. Yet, despite the familiar landmarks, Roth still wasn't really certain how long it would take him to reach the urn. The vision itself had seemed to take scant minutes, but Roth knew that more than a half an hour had passed before he had come to his senses and risen to leave the cave. Now as he inched along, clattering the jetpack over rows of stalactites and raining them down onto his shoulders, he realized that he was walking a lot further than he had originally intended. He wondered just how deep into the caves he would have to go.

The depths of the Corridors had never been fully explored. They had been located in 2052 by a low orbiting satellite, originally performing earth-surface echoes in search of potential petroleum reserves. Svalbard and the surrounding seabed had yielded a variety of promising drilling sites. They had also reflected—from the island of Nordaustlandet, specifically—a cluster of impulses indicating a vast network of subterranean passageways.

Evidence of the passageways existed on the satellite field-scans for twelve years or more without arousing much interest. (After all, the oil companies were bent on drilling, not spelunking.) But in 2064, the University of Oslo petitioned some of the scans for use in a geological density survey. The faculty took one look at the impulse readings along the southeast coast of Nordaustlandet and organized an expedition on the spot.

The jetpack was causing trouble now, scraping and squealing against the tunnel walls, finally wedging tight as Roth navigated a fissure. He braced his hands solidly and shoved himself loose with a backward lurch. Then he shed the pack, attached the rope and towed it carefully behind.

Once the Norwegians had arrived on the island, it had taken them nearly three weeks to locate the mouth of the caverns, which had been sealed over by advancing glaciers. But when they finally melted their way in with neutron charges, the explorers found all of their time and effort well worthwhile. The caves were a masterpiece of natural handiwork, a sprawling network of limestone chambers and ice forests. Formed eons before, when receding glaciers had given way to warm, primordial seas, the passageways had been carved by an interconnecting system of underground rivers. By now referred to as the "Nordaustlandet Corridors," they weaved for more than fifty miles under the glacier field, one of the longest natural cave systems in the world.

Yet the Norwegians' geological discoveries represented little more than a fraction of the treasures eventually to be uncovered in the Corridors. Because, as the explorers soon learned, the caves also contained evidence of an ancient civilization—one that had existed for perhaps a hundred years before its inhabitants had utterly and inexplicably . . .

Roth was falling.

Puffing from exertion, he had rammed himself through another icy fissure and turned back to guide the jetpack, momentarily forgetting the deep chasm that lay at the end of the narrow passage. Now, suddenly, there was nothing under his feet.

. . . falling, merciful Heaven I'm falling into the pit!

He wrenched his body around in blind terror, flailing for something besides empty air. The laserflare jumped from his grasp. For a split second, suspended in slow motion, he watched it fall . . . and fall . . . and fall . . . down into the maw of a gaping abyss, like Gepetto's lantern hurtling into the belly of the whale. With breathless horror, Roth realized that his own body was tumbling close behind. His scream roared around him, echoing and re-echoing.

Then something jerked him to a swaying stop.

It was the line to the jet pack, still locked reflexively in his fists. Somewhere above him the pack must have lodged in the rocks.

How tight is it?

Or how loose?

He hung in absolute blackness. His heart thundered in his ears. The only light anywhere in his world was the tiny, ember-like dot of the laserflare that had bounded into the rocks at the floor of the pit.

Roth clung viciously to the rope—small, so small, almost lost in the padding of his thermogloves—scarcely substantial enough to feel, let alone to grip for dear life. In the deathly silence, with only his raging heartbeat to keep him company, Roth could hear the rope rasping, creaking, slipping slowly through his glove grasp.

He kicked into the surrounding darkness, swinging his feet in gentle, shuddering arcs.

The pack. The pack is up there, and it's just barely hanging on, and if I move too fast or too hard or too much I'm going to jerk it loose I'm going to rip it down I'm going to fall I'm going to die.

A terse cry escaped his lips. Again his feet tested the darkness, twice, three times. Nothing. He was dangling free over the pit, totally blind, on a half-anchored rope that was even now creeping out of his grip. And suddenly, insanely, his nose itched.

Roth's mind raced, like a rat scurrying for escape from a hot oven. But the door was shut tight. No cracks. The rat's mouth gaped, squeaking hoarse and dry. Except that it wasn't the rat at all. It was the rope, squeaking slowly but surely against his gloves, inching out of his hands.

Roth prayed. He pleaded for his life in terrified mental bursts that scrolled through his brain like data racing at lightspeed over a terminal screen. Finally the pleas escaped out of clenched teeth. There was only enough breath for two words.

"God . . . help! . . . "

And even as he spoke, he felt something smack against the sole of his swinging snow boot. He reached out wildly, kicking for it again, flailing what seemed like a full circle before finally connecting. And what he felt was a rocky wall, apparently hidden before by his own panic, dry enough and rough enough to give his foot a fleeting purchase.

Roth grappled with his feet. Lunging, he jerked his left fist into a grip above the right.

Something overhead groaned and buckled.

Roth bobbed on the rope for an endless second, fully expecting to feel his tense weight suddenly released into space. But the rope settled and held firm.

Thank you, Father, oh thank you.

With a savage grunt, Roth began climbing. He whipped his right hand to the top position. Then the left. Then right. His feet groped and clambered, now and again jarring a stone loose and sending it into a long silence from which it would finally reverberate with a hollow crack. Sweat drizzled into the corners of his blind eyes, burning. His breath came in short, groaning gasps. Then, suddenly, his right hand shot out for the rope and found stone.

He was at the top.

He skittered his glove across the rock like a bug on a hot plate, finally stubbing his fingers into a handhold. Roth gave a mighty tug, heaving his body upward with an awkward half-leap. The ledge hit him in the middle of the rib cage, threatening to slide away again. He slid his hand haltingly along the rope, extending his arm. Then he hitched his body upward once more. He plopped onto his belly, finally there to stay, a jagged rock fragment punching deep into his foams and jabbing him hard just above the groin.

It was just possibly the most wonderful feeling he had ever had in his life.

Clawing and rolling, Roth scrambled the rest of the way onto the ledge. Then he just lay in the darkness, half laughing and half crying, clinging to the jet pack.

Wiping some tears away, he scratched his nose.

Laserflares bulged under the jetpack cover. Roth slipped his hand inside and extracted one, snapping it to life. He had craved light nearly as much as solid ground, and now he basked in the glow, glancing around, verifying the fact that he really *was* still alive and breathing and resting his terrorized muscles on something that could support his whole weight.

Then he froze.

He stared at the drop-off tight-lipped. At first he was confused, then incredulous, then awe-struck with complete realization. Fresh tears welled in his eyes.

There was nothing there. No broad crack. No rocky projections. Nothing but a flat ledge and a handful of low, jagged, groin-punching stones. Nothing for the jetpack to catch on and hold. Absolutely nothing.

Challenges await thee. And dangers. But He will guide and protect thee . . .

All at once the presence of the cave, huge and quiet, rose around him, and Roth felt extremely small. He drew himself to his knees, hung his head and prayed. The tears flowed openly.

8

At the same moment that Roth had first materialized on the pad outside the entrance to the Corridors, Roald Hoeksberg had lain in the throes of what he might have described later as a nightmare, had he been able to remember it.

He found himself back at the university, at the door of a sumptuous administrative office that he had never seen before. The office was quite dark, but he could still make out a few details. The furniture was lushly padded. Several framed art pieces—they appeared to be Durer's etchings from Dante's *Divine Comedy*—lined the walls. At the far end of the room, from behind a thick desk, a man looked up.

"Come in, Roald," he invited. "Please come in."

The man was little more than a dim shape, cloaked in the shadows of the room. He beckoned with a shadow of a hand.

Roald stepped inside. He drew a coat collar up around his neck. The room was uncomfortably cold. The Shadow-man made a magnanimous gesture toward a chair by his desk.

"Make yourself at home," he said. The voice was barely more than an emotionless whisper, but it hissed with piercing force. It was a voice that Hoeksberg didn't like very well. No, not at all. In fact, he had a sudden urge to flee from that voice, to turn and charge out the door without so much as a glance over his shoulder, to run and run and run until he was miles away.

He stepped softly to the chair and sat.

The Shadowman smiled. To Hoeksberg's eyes it was nothing more than a subtle swelling of shadow cheeks. But it sent a shiver rippling up from his belly and over his chest.

"We must talk about Roth," the Shadowman said. "What are we going to do about him, you and me?"

"Do about him? . . . " Hoeksberg's voice was half air. He swallowed and his throat clicked.

"He is a troublemaker, Roald. You've seen that from the beginning. He's a boat-rocker. A rule-breaker. He doesn't give one whit about your research, about all of the time and back-breaking effort you've spent to secure funding and establish connections. He's out for his own glory, and that alone. Mr. Derek Roth, hustling for Number One."

Hoeksberg nodded. His heart was still pounding, but the crawl of his flesh was starting to subside. Because he could see that what the Shadowman was saying was true. Yes. What the Shadowman said made perfect sense, and perfect sense always displaced fear. That was a scientific truism.

"Your researchers are an admirable team, Roald. They work hard. They follow your leadership. Roth wants no part of that team. His motives are totally self-centered. And his influence is spreading. Look at what he is doing to the girl, McKesson. One of your own interns! You are losing her to him. She used to burn with enthusiasm for your work. Now she would rather sit and dote over his. You have noticed this, haven't you?"

He had.

"She is behind in her cataloging," Hoeksberg agreed. "She has been for over a week."

"Which of the others will be next?"

Hoeksberg shifted in his seat. McKesson obviously had some sort of attachment for Roth, and until now Hoeksberg had tolerated it to a degree. But the thought of others following suit had never ocurred to him. It was not a pleasant possibility.

"All of these things are true, aren't they Roald? I am simply expressing feelings that you have had yourself, feelings that you have had all along. Am I right?"

He was. He was precisely, uncannily right.

"Consider his entire attitude. Does he offer you respect? Hmm? Like the others. Oh, no no no no. Certainly not. He addresses you by your *first name*, Roald. This contemptible little man regards himself as your *equal*! An insolent upstart without the least regard for protocol! Without the slightest inkling of the associations you share, the power you possess!"

Hoeksberg snorted scornfully. "He's a nobody! A fool..!"

"A fool has no respect for power, Roald. You and I have it. It doesn't come easy, no, but we have *earned* it. Men like Roth would just as soon take it all away.

"Who received the better press, Roald? Who caught the eye of the media when they visited the island last summer?"

Hoeksberg darkened. Roth had. His gene scanning monstrosity had made international headlines. The only international coverage Hoeksberg got was that vile rubbish in the Enquirer.

"At this very moment he is plotting against you, Roald. He is defying your very instructions, pursuing his own selfish ends, lying in wait for the right opportunity to seize even more of those rewards which are not rightfully his. Rewards that belong to you."

"To me," Hoeksberg repeated. And rage churned deep inside him. Full-blown, indignant rage.

"We must not allow this to go on, Roald. We must stop men like him, you and me. Or we will lose everything we have worked so hard for. So long for."

At that moment something scuttled across the dark desk top. Without effort the Shadowman plucked it up and displayed it, its silhouette legs wriggling madly. A roach perhaps. Hoeksberg didn't care. His rage consumed him.

"He is dross," the Shadowman hissed. "Mere vermin. *Crush* him, Roald. Crush him *now*."

There was a papery crunch. The wriggling legs instantly jutted, quivered, froze.

"For you, for a man of power, it will be as easy as this."

The insect fell from the shadow hand, clicking onto the desk top.

Hoeksberg nodded with savage resolve. He could feel the power now, flowing into his veins: a cool, pounding fury like the beat of some enormous, eternal machine. He felt infinite strength, infinite authority, infinite control.

He felt like the Shadowman.

And the next morning when he awoke, although he would remember nothing of the dream, Hoeksberg would still feel the same way.

9

Roth glanced at his chronometer, his lips tight. It was already 10:00 AM. He set back to work on the urn.

The chamber housing it was enormous. Its cathedral ceiling stretched overhead for hundreds of feet like the underside of some giant pincushion, needled solid with stalactites. They grew longer and healthier toward the far reaches of the cavern, finally meeting the floor in a thick grove of limestone columns. The floor was terraced with flowing ice and stone, which descended step by step to create a natural amphitheater. Center stage was a wide, frozen pool laced with feathers of frost.

Roth scarcely noticed. He hunched over the urn, the jetpack still strapped to his back. His hands moved quickly but carefully, chiseling permafrost, loosening and ejecting stones, sweeping away the ice-dust and starting again. The clay vessel was more than half-exposed now, showing ten distinct bands of shiny metal ringing its midsection. Although pitted and stained with age, the urn was large and whole, free of the slightest crack. A drop of sweat fell from Roth's chin and splattered quick-frozen on the urn's neck. He was late, and he was worried.

He had spent most of the night on the ledge, repairing the jetpack.

Roth wiped his wet face with a forearm and set to chiseling again. Jetpack repair was not exactly his specialty, and it had taken him more than an hour merely to locate the problem. The casing of the pack had taken some nasty dents when he had dropped over the ledge. One of the dents was deep enough to pinch off three little alloy tubes that sat right over the top of a the big elliptical thing in the middle of the whole works—whatever that was. Anyway, it had taken a combination of teeth, fingernails, small rocks and the air tractor key (fortunately he had forgotten to remove it earlier from the pouch in his foams) to coax the little bounders into operation again. It had also taken four and a half hours.

Now, with the urn all but exposed, Roth's thoughts jumped back and forth between his work and the scene he knew must be unfolding at the compound. He was absent from the lounge at breakfast time, and then from the morning briefing at nine. By now they all probably knew that he was nowhere to be found inside the building. If they had been perceptive enough to check the digiport compulog, they would have discovered that some body left for the Corridor pad at approximately two-thirty that morning. It would take very little deduction to ascertain that he was the somebody in question. Hoeksberg would be upset. More precisely, he would be foaming at the mouth. Fortunately, the wind was probably still going strong, and that meant Hoeksberg couldn't send anyone out after him.

Roth flicked a pebble from beneath the belly of the urn and all at once it popped loose with a resonant *tonk*! He lifted it free and held it up, gazing at it with a mixture of awe and triumph. The first step in his errand was fulfilled.

Roth centered the jetpack on his back, cradled the urn in his arms, and headed out of the chamber. Within an hour he would be back at the mouth of the Corridors. Ten minutes more and he would be materializing at the center of the compound's main digiport pad. Whatever else the future might hold for him could only be faced with faithful resignation.

Remain faithful. Be patient and take heart.
I'm doing my best, Father, believe me . . .

But despite his efforts, Roth could feel the apprehension building, starting with a sick throb at the base of his throat.

* * *

And for good reason. Hoeksberg was already waiting.

10

Lee paced quietly outside the door to Hoeksberg's quarters, not wanting to be heard but wanting desperately to hear. She had been one of the real-life players in Roth's mental scenario, noting with growing alarm his absence from the lounge, from the briefing and, finally, from his own quarters. Now she passed back and forth in front of Hoeksberg's office, where the two men sat inside, trying to catch what she could of the second act. Her steps were stiff, her mouth dry. She was scared to death for Roth. His unauthorized trip to the digs had sent Hoeksberg into a rage. And Hoeksberg had too much power in the academic community to dismiss his wrath lightly.

But that wasn't all that worried her. What scared Lee the most was Roth himself. Her fears now went beyond the fleeting glassiness in his eyes. Ignoring the wind-chill and digiporting to the Corridors had been an unbelievably dangerous move. Either Roth had some valid reason for it, or he was becoming irrational. And from the sounds of things on the other side of the door, if Roth *had* a valid reason he sure wasn't sharing it with Hoeksberg. That in *itself* was irrational. Because if there was one thing Roth needed right now, it was a good excuse.

Lee glanced both ways down the hallway and passed closer to the door again. Worry wrapped her like a damp cloak. She stood quiet and listened.

* * *

Inside the room, Roth sat expressionless. The night had left him visibly exhausted. He scanned a three-page form in his lap while Hoeksberg stood, eyeing him coolly. Somewhere inside his face a dark smile was lurking, waiting to surface.

The surroundings were stark and businesslike, much more like an office than normal sleeping quarters. And perhaps it was only the fatigue, but Roth detected an uncomfortable chill in the room as if Hoeksberg had intentionally cranked down the heat. The overall effect was decidedly un-homey and, Roth thought, deliberately intimidating.

He glanced up from the form, too incredulous to be indignant.

"You can't do this," he said. Even as he spoke, he remembered the urgency he had felt the night before, the compulsion to retrieve the urn without delay. Now everything made perfect sense.

"It is already done, Mr. Roth," Hoeksberg said. "Dean Wells has pledged his signature. Frank Mirisch has already opened a slot for you in his Brazilian expedition. I spoke with him only this morning. He is counting on your assistance." With that the smile broke loose. It reeked with patronage. And something else, something poisonous and wicked like the fangs of a viper. Despite a long history of run-ins with Hoeksberg, Roth had never seen a smile like that before. He felt a simultaneous rush of anger and apprehension. He held both in check.

"This isn't the army, Roald. You can't just transfer me to some other project like a grunt fresh out of basic. I've spent nearly two years here. So what now? Scrap all my data, chuck all the findings and head for Brazil?"

"You needn't be concerned. We will make sufficient use of all your findings."

Roth felt his face flush with rage. "I'll bet. And when you present them in your next paper, you'll be sure to mention my name, won't you?"

Hoeksberg's smile faded, but the poison remained, like a stain. "Dr. Mirisch is leaving within ten days," he stated quietly. "You are cleared to digiport back to the main pad at the university tomorrow morning at eight o' clock. There you will attend a preparatory briefing. We will box up your equipment and ship it at the earliest convenience."

"You can't do this to me, Roald," Roth repeated. He straightened slowly in his chair, his face tight, his thoughts racing. He had managed to stash the urn among some other artifacts awaiting a scan in the corner of the main digiport bay. At this point, he wasn't sure exactly what his next step was supposed to be, but he *was* sure of one thing. By rule of law, all artifacts discovered in the Corridors belonged to the Norwegian government. If he had to return to the university, there was no way in the world he could take the urn with him. And if he took too long getting back to Nordaustlandet, the urn might very well end up in a crate headed for Oslo. If that happened, he would almost certainly never see it again.

He pointed a finger into Hoeksberg's chest. "You're *not* going to do this to me," he amended furiously. "You're totally out of line, and I'll scream clear up to the president's office!"

The hideous smile returned. "You forget," Hoeksberg snarled, "that you have violated the regulations of the Institute on a regular basis." His eyes were black glass, cold and sharp. "I have more than enough evidence to, shall we say, *convict* you. Your screams will fall on deaf ears."

Roth glared silently. His heart pounded. The cold pressed on him like a stone.

"My researchers are an admirable team, Mr. Roth. They work hard, they follow my leadership. You want no part of that team, because your motives are totally self-centered. You are a trouble-maker, Mr. Roth. From the very beginning you have defied my instructions, pursued your own selfish ends." His smile was widening now, twisting grotesquely. Roth stared back, his chest thudding. Something about Hoeksberg was suddenly incredibly revolting. Any second, he thought. Any second the fangs will appear, and the gray, forked tongue will dart, quivering.

"And your trip to the caves during the night," Hoeksberg went on. "A hunch, you say? Intuition. Following up on a wild hare, hmmm? No, Mr. Roth. Those are not explanations. Those are evasions. It is quite clear to me that you were doing something at the site, something behind my back. And in the process you committed your most flagrant violation of all. You could be transferred from this project on the basis of that infraction alone . . . "

With that, despite his exhaustion, Roth was on his feet, his eyes burning. He cut Hoeksberg off abruptly. "That 'transfer' doesn't have one blessed thing to do with what happened last night and you know it! You've had it in the works ever since the media coverage last summer, haven't you Roald? And why? Because in those *decent* features in the Times and the Post, *my* name showed up more often than yours! The gene scan was their main peg. And *your* biggest coverage was in the Inquirer. Isn't that it, Roald? Didn't that stick in your craw? Taking a back seat to a non-vested peon from the zoology department?"

Roth glared unflinching into Hoeksberg's eyes. Hoeksberg stared back, his jaw muscles clenched like fists. He spoke with quiet venom.

"I'm going to crush you, Mr. Roth," he said, and his words rang with hateful determination. "I'm going to crumple your entire career into a small, ragged wad and stuff it into the corner of some dim little basement office crammed to the ceiling with freshman midterms. No more overpriced gadgetry. No more resplendent publicity. No more *research*, period. I'm going to reduce you to *nothing*, Mr. Roth. In very short order. The process has already begun."

Roth did not blink. Even for Hoeksberg, that was a pretty stiff threat, and Roth doubted that he could pull it off. But he could try, and even that was enough to send an electric shiver up Roth's spine. However, it wasn't enough to make him back down. Not now.

"Try it," Roth shot back, struggling fiercely to keep his voice low and controlled.

Hoeksberg breathed a dry laugh. But Roth's gaze held firm, and Hoeksberg's black sneer slowly sucked back into his face. "You have packing to do," he said. "I suggest you return to your room and begin."

They stood for a moment, staring each other down.

"Keep your hands off my equipment," Roth said. " I'll come back for it myself."

"I'm afraid you won't be coming back, Mr. Roth," Hoeksberg returned. There was an unsettling confidence in his voice. Roth set his jaw.

"We'll see," he said. He jerked the door open, stalked out and slammed it behind him.

He nearly knocked Lee onto the floor. She made a little gasping sound and stumbled backward, her eyes wide with surprise and embarrassment. Roth was just as startled. He started to speak, intending to excuse himself, not yet taking the time to wonder what she had been doing there.

Then something came into his head—something strong and sudden—that told him to do otherwise. The instructions were instantaneous and precise, and he followed them like a reflex. He grabbed Lee by the shoulders, restoring her balance and hustling her down the hallway. Shushing her quietly, he led her around a corner out of earshot from Hoeksberg and steered her toward his own quarters. Despite all of his earlier bravado, it was now clear to Roth that he was headed for home. And it might be quite a while before he would be able to return to Nordaustlandet. That being the case, he had a lot to tell Lee before morning.

She was going to have to take over for him.

11

Lee sat silently on Roth's bed, her hands folded on her knees, watching him line the bottom of an old trunk with books and journals and dogeared data pads. He moved with obvious effort. He had already told her about the urn and its discovery: the brief, visionary flashes culminating in what he now referred to as the flight through the cave; the voice that had awakened him; that same voice recurring in the dream; the miraculous rescue above the pit.

"I couldn't tell you anything last night," he apologized tiredly. "Didn't know what was happening, really. I thought . . . I don't know. Could have been losing my mind." He turned to her with a bleak smile. "It's hard to describe the feeling . . . crazy . . . "

Lee just nodded. She had been listening quietly, asking few questions, studying Roth's every move. Because what he was saying was so incredibly bizarre. Crazy. That was the word she had kept thinking of herself.

Maybe Roth *was* going crazy . . .

She had actually considered the possibility at first. He had related everything so matter-of-factly. As if this were simply another one of those times you hear about where inspiration guides somebody to locate one of those mysterious ancient urns. In fact, Roth's tone had reminded her a little of those religious weirdos with the funny haircuts that wandered around the commercial digiport terminals.

He padded to the bed, rummaging through the clutter spread there. He shook his head.

"And the incredible thing," Roth continued, "is that I still don't know *why*. I don't have the slightest idea what all this is for." He stopped and looked up at her, now quite earnest. "But I do know one thing. You're supposed to know. You're meant to be in on this. I felt that just as sure as anything as soon as I saw you in the hallway."

She stared at him. Any doubts she might have had regarding Roth's sanity were already melting away. Because as she watched him, what she saw in Roth's eyes—behind the dull weariness—was that old familiar rationality. And something else as well, something that shamed her just a little. It was trust. After all, she was his friend. And they shared the gospel. She, of all people, should know where he was coming from. Certainly, she would understand . . . wouldn't she?

Roth squinted at her.

"What were you doing outside that door anyway?"

Lee felt a half-blush. She let out a sigh and gazed at him defiantly. "I was eavesdropping. What did you think?"

He went back to rummaging, nodding faintly.

"That's what I thought."

"I was concerned about you," she explained defensively. "I didn't know whether Hoeksberg was going to send you back to the university to have you drawn and quartered, or do it right there in his office with a letter opener or something. I had to find out."

Roth smiled drily. "He went with option A."

Lee smiled back. Yes, she was beginning to understand. These were pearls that Roth wouldn't have cast in just anyone's direction. He hadn't breathed a single word to Hoeksberg, even though his career was on the line. And because of that—if for no other reason—Lee felt duty-bound to listen with an open mind.

"Where is it now?" she heard herself ask. "The urn . . . is it here someplace?" She realized that her heart was beating faster than normal. No, she wasn't just considering the truthfulness of Roth's story now. Now she was accepting it. Moreover, she was *feeling* it. Something warm and calm was touching her heart, bringing a growing assurance.

"I snuck it in with Wong's pots," Roth groaned. He gave up on his rummaging and plopped down in the middle of the heap. "That big bunch over behind the fragment crates, waiting for a scan. I didn't want Hoeksberg to see it."

That was easy to understand. There had been bad blood brewing between the two for quite some time. Now Hoeksberg was apt to stir up all the trouble he could muster. Roth let out an exhausted breath and rubbed his face. Lee could hear the unshaven whiskers scrubbing his palms. That feeling of assurance was brimming now, swelling to force out all doubt.

"You'll have to hide it better than that," he said. "Scan it with the rest of the stuff and then get it out of there. Keep it safe. I don't even know what we're supposed to do with it yet, and we can't afford to let it get shipped." He had said "we" just as matter-of-factly as everything else. Lee accepted it just as simply. She was irrevocably part of things now, the feeling told her so. Still, she didn't allow herself to think too far ahead.

"Where?" she asked. "Any ideas?"

Roth fell back on the bed, his hand over his forehead. A pile of scientific journals slid and scrunched under his back. "Uh . . . well . . . " he began, and she realized that he was fighting a losing battle against his eyelids. He looked up, and his eyes found hers. He never finished the thought.

"I'm sorry, Lee. I'm sorry to do this to you."

She felt a rush of emotion, so strong that it brought a momentary light-headedness. He hadn't called her Lee since their first few days on the digs. Her name, formed in the deep tones of his tired voice, sounded better than she ever would have imagined.

"You can't be sorry," she returned. "It isn't your doing anyway. Not if what you say is true—and I believe it is."

Inexplicably, tears welled in her eyes.

Roth squeezed her hand.

"You're really something. You know that?"

She smiled back. His face swam in her eyes.

"Ditto."

And then he became somber. He took her hand in both of his, cradling it dearly.

"Be careful with Hoeksberg," he warned. "There's something about him. I can't quite put my finger on it." He gazed dully at the ceiling, trying to frame the thought. "He seems . . . bad . . . dangerous . . . " He looked back at her, unsatisfied. The words had obviously escaped him. "Just be careful. Will you?"

She nodded uneasily. Then she remembered the urn.

"The hiding place. For the urn. You had an idea? . . . "

"Uh . . . " His red eyes narrowed. "Uh . . . no." He looked up at her bleakly and smiled. "Maybe you ought to pray about it." He squeezed her hand once more, and within seconds sleep overcame him.

Lee gazed down at him. He looked pitiful. His hair poked every which way into the magazine pages crumpled at the crown of his head. Whiskers darkened his face. The wrinkles at the corners of his eyes cut his face with deep, humorless lines. She reached over and brushed the salt and pepper back from his forehead, as she had thought about doing so many times before. Then she leaned down and kissed him, pressing her lips gently against the rugged warmth of his mouth. He stirred only slightly.

She sat staring at him for a long time after that, her thoughts and emotions whirlpooling, cycling between wild anticipation and desperate anxiety. Finally she pulled off his shoes, heaved his legs up onto the bunk and drew a blanket over his chest.

Then she went back to her room and followed his advice.

II
Whispers From The Dust

12

Some thirty-six hours later, Lee found herself sitting in the cool darkness of the digiport bay with only her thoughts to keep her company. She stared into Roth's terminal screen, watching the cursor blink a slow trail along an irregular scan path. Out on the scannerbot grid sat a cluster of pots and fragments. Just right of dead center was Roth's urn, peering nonchalantly over the handles of one of Wong's clay jars. The scannerbot hummed and swiveled through the artifacts. Finishing an examination of a fissured half-moon that looked like the leftovers from some sort of ancient cereal bowl, the scannerbot drew in its arm with a whirring snap, pirouetted on the grid, and telescoped the scan head toward the base of Roth's urn. With a mechanical whine the arm set to work, arcing first left and then right like a sideways pendulum, moving from bottom to top. Lee winced at the noise and glanced back at the door. Now that Roth was gone, the last thing she needed was to attract some curious co-workers.

She gazed out toward the pad where Roth had disappeared in a flash of light particles only that morning. Already she missed him desperately. She had spent the better part of two semesters by his side: working, talking, sharing hours and hours of successes and frustrations and scores of other mutual feelings. How could she possibly have failed to notice, until scarcely a day and a half ago, that she had been slowly but surely falling in love with him the entire time? His sudden absence confirmed all of her feelings in one fell swoop, and now they pierced deep inside her, filling her with bittersweet longing. She had no idea when she would be able to see him again.

Lee watched the scannerbot spin. She felt small and alone, face to face with a task she scarcely understood, yet somehow knew to be monumentally important. Her prayers had revealed that much to her, in a general way, even though they had left her pretty much in the dark regarding details.

Well, most of the details. She *had* gotten some impressions on concealing the urn. After a lot of thought and a little scrounging she had located a microchip transmitter among some of the spelunking equipment in general storage. Tonight after everyone was asleep, she would place the transmitter in the urn, wrap it in canvas and bury it in the snow on the drift-side of the compound. When the time came to find it again, the signal from the transmitter would guide the way.

Suddenly the terminal beeped. Lee started, clunking her knee under the table. Then she looked up. The cursor bipped across the screen like a tiny comet, trailing data. The scan head had found something.

She looked out at the grid. The robot arm was poised in mid-pass over the belly of the urn, about four inches up from the bottom. It hovered there for just a second or two, then resumed the scan. Left behind on the screen were three and a half lines of letters, numbers and geometric symbols. Probably some kind of mold, Lee thought. Or a fungus. Not enough data there for anything larger. And whatever it was, it was old. Most molds and fungus registered live data. This data was slack.

Lee had to smile to herself, remembering how maladroit she had felt during her first attempts at running the scanner. Roth had teased her ceaselessly back then. Now she was a walking instruction manual, complete with glossary. *Slack data: characterized by simple chromatin junctures, yielding defunct clone. Live data: characterized by complex chromatin junctures, yielding viable clone.*

Or, to put it more simply, slack data came from organic material long since dead. And when you sent it through to the pad, it materialized as something dead. Neat and complete, perfect in every detail, but dead as a doornail.

On the other hand, live data came from organic material that was either preserved or still reasonably fresh. And when you sent it through to the pad, you came up with a living organism. That didn't happen very often, except with things like lichens and molds. Once it happened with a woolly mammoth, and the damage had been extensive. Roth should have known better. But he had allowed his professional curiosity to get the better of him, and he had come close to paying very dearly for it. Hoeksberg nearly managed to shut him down over the incident. After that, official policy prohibited materializing live clones. And that was one policy that Roth respected judiciously.

"The hour is growing late, Miss McKesson."

Lee froze. The voice came from directly behind her. It was Hoeksberg's.

"And you've only finished half of your cataloging. You'll have quite a lengthy job ahead of you in the morning, don't you think?" Jealousy prowled in his voice. She recognized it immediately, and she knew why it was there. She was working on Roth's project, not his.

"I was just finishing some of these up," she said, looking over her shoulder as nonchalantly as she could. She felt about as nonchalant as the San Francisco Earthquake. "Dr. Wong left them here three days ago. I can finish the cataloging tomorrow, before breakfast." She swallowed, her mouth suddenly very dry.

She had seen Hoeksberg earlier, during the day. But she hadn't actually spoken to him, or even passed close enough to share a glance. Now Hoeksberg's face loomed out of the darkness, glowing rich yellow in the light of the computer screen. He was smiling. It was the most unpleasant smile she had ever seen. All at once it reminded her of the hungry smile of Bela Lugosi, leering from the dark corridors of an ancient 2-D video she had viewed once.

Be careful with Hoeksberg . . . there's something about him . . . he seems bad . . . dangerous . . .

"Mmmm," he grunted, his smile unwavering. He sidled closer to her and cast a steely gaze out toward the grid, eyes glinting. Lee instinctively leaned away, not wanting him close, not even wanting him within reaching distance. She suppressed the urge to follow his gaze, to sneak a peek at the urn and see how much of it was actually showing.

"You know, of course," Hoeksberg cooed blackly, "that Mr. Roth's phase of our project is now finished."

Lee nodded. Her voice wanted to quaver but she held it even. "Yes. But since these were scheduled to be scanned before he left, I thought . . . " She shrugged stiffly. She didn't know what the heck she thought, because she didn't have a single good reason for completing the scan. Except that Roth told her to do the urn.

Hoeksberg was still looking out toward it.

"Your involvement with this phase of the project is finished as well," he went on. "I will be dismantling this equipment and shipping it to the university at the earliest possible convenience. Its usefulness to us here is marginal at best, and your time could be spent much more profitably in pursuits contributing to the completion of your project. Don't you agree?"

In spite of the irrational trembling in her chest, Lee bristled.

Marginally useful! Anything that doesn't contribute directly to your personal aggrandizement is only marginally useful, isn't it? You contemptible, egotistical! . . .

Her mind screamed it at him, but when her lips moved, they said simply: "I'll finish the cataloging in the morning. Don't worry."

She wanted the lights on, and she wanted them on right this minute. She didn't like being here with him in the dark. He was standing close now, looking directly down on top of her. That leering yellow face, like a sinister parody of the man in the moon.

"Oh, I don't worry," he said, and teeth blossomed in his smile. "You will complete what is expected, I am quite certain of it."

She smiled back, very tightly. "Yes," she said.

He turned to leave, and then turned back, as if to give her an aside. He put a hand on her shoulder and her muscles flinched. Even through her clothing, the hand was cold. Ice cold.

"In Mr. Roth's absence, I consider this equipment to be my responsibility. In the interest of preventing damage, after tonight I am placing it strictly off limits to all personnel. You'll be sure and pass the word along, won't you?"

"Certainly." She kept her eyes straight ahead. She didn't want to look up into that face again. No, not now.

"Thank you." His voice had an air of finality, but the icy grip on her shoulder remained. He glanced out toward the grid one last time.

"And incidentally, not all of those artifacts are from Dr. Wong's group, are they?"

Lee felt something jump sharply in her chest. It must have shown on her face, because Hoeksberg's smile widened immediately.

"The tall one, with the bands. That was the one Mr. Roth brought back from the digs yesterday morning. Wasn't it?"

Lee felt herself go white. How could he possibly have known? Roth hadn't even hinted at it during their conversation. And she had scarcely spoken to Hoeksberg for the last two days. But then, that wouldn't have made any difference. Hoeksberg had smelled something in the air, and somehow he had tracked it down. Maybe Wong had spied the urn among the fragments. Or maybe one of the students had spotted Roth with it when he first came in. Whatever. At any rate, Hoeksberg knew it was there. And he undoubtedly knew that Roth had tried to hide it from him.

The grip on her shoulder was tightening.

Lee turned toward the grid, pushing all of the expression from her face with supreme effort. She raised her eyebrows.

"Was it?" she asked.

Hoeksberg's fist was vise-tight now, cold as bone. Lee could feel herself trembling beneath it.

"As soon as you are finished here, Miss McKesson, I would like to have that piece in my office." His voice was sharp, in perfect synergy with his fingers, which were bearing down, digging in. Lee felt a cry rise into her throat. Around her the very air seemed to chill. It curled around her face like an obscene caress.

"Tonight," he repeated. "I will be waiting."

Lee nodded dumbly, tensing against a scream, and abruptly the grip relaxed. Only a moment later Hoeksberg was gone, the door echoing shut behind him.

She heaved a great, quivering breath and slid a hand to her shoulder. The chill clung, lightened, finally faded to a vague memory as she rubbed the ache away. She gazed out at Roth's urn, stricken. It was now Hoeksberg's, and there would be no way to get it back. All of her elaborate plans had just evaporated into thin air. Her eyes welled uncontrollably.

That was when the computer went crazy.

Still half-dazed, Lee turned to the screen. She stared at it dully for a moment while it beeped and hummed, her brain trying to shift gears. Then her eyes grew wide. She hurled a glance out at the grid.

The scannerbot circled and spun like a twentieth-century jitterbug, weaving tight rotations around the urn. Alternately stretching and contracting, the scanner arm held the head in precise position, locked into an orbit over the lowest of the urn's metal bands. It wound around again and again, riding slowly from one edge toward the other—almost, Lee realized later, as if it were tracking a disc.

And on the monitor, sped to a blur, the cursor shot madly from left to right, scrolling data so fast that Lee could just barely see it. Filling screen after screen after screen.

The first microdisc was full after just three minutes. Lee popped it from the drive and jammed in another. Forty seconds into the fifth disc, the scannerhead jumped directly to the next band on the urn and started all over again. The robot screamed, its arm clicking and pumping over the third, the fourth, the fifth bands. Lee tore open another carton of microdiscs. The scannerhead raced on. Band six, seven, eight.

Nine.

Ten.

The cursor beeped perfunctorily and spit up into the corner of the screen, which emptied in the blink of an eye. The entire process had taken nearly two hours. Lee brushed the hair out of her face. She gathered the scattered discs from around the keyboard and drive unit, counting as she went. There were forty seven.

Forty-seven full discs.

Full of what?

She felt a shiver ripple down her neck. The data had crossed the screen too fast for her to see many details. But after watching it hit the monitor for two solid hours, she was certain of at least one thing. It was linked with complex chromatin junctures.

It was live data.

Lee's thoughts swirled. She had to talk to Roth.

She hid the discs safely away under her bunk before heading for Hoeksberg's quarters. Treading the warm brilliance of the compound's well-lit hallway, the unpleasantness of her earlier encounter seemed to blur. By the time she had reached his doorway, she found herself wondering just what had been real and what had been imagination. Hoeksberg was an ogre of sorts to be sure, but envisioning him in the same league as Count Dracula had been going just a bit too far, now hadn't it? When Hoeksberg answered her knock, looking much more tired than demonic, she decided in the affirmative. Even so, she was glad the lights were on in the hallway.

After delivering the urn she excused herself brusquely, returned to her room and dug through a heap and a half of old syllabi. Finally she found a course introduction sheet with Roth's home phone number on it. Stealing into the communication cube at the north end of the lounge, she grabbed a portable SATCOM—a satellite communicator—and placed a direct call.

Half a world away, Roth's pictophone buzzed rhythmically in the silence of his empty apartment. Lee listened to the sound repeat in her earpiece, first waiting, then wishing, finally giving up.

* * *

In the meantime, oblivious to her efforts, Hoeksberg was settling into an uneasy sleep. Somewhere, in a dark office beyond his waking memory, he was about to receive additional instructions.

13

Hoeksberg had returned to his room from the digiport bay feeling curiously drained. He felt grouchy. No, *vicious*. Lately, it seemed, he had been that way a lot. He had also been tired: not just physically tired, but mentally tired, his emotions stretched and spent. It was almost as if some huge, invisible taskmaster were riding his shoulders, loading him down.

He knew what was wrong. He had been feeling this way ever since his confrontation with Roth. Roth was an insolent upstart without the slightest regard for protocol. Roth had done this to him, and Roth was going to pay.

Somewhere, in the back of his mind, Hoeksberg knew quite clearly that Roth had been plotting against him. Hoeksberg knew how those things worked. He was an old plotter from way back. He had plotted against the best of them. And he had invariably come out ahead. Over the last couple of days, though, he had felt himself slipping. He hadn't felt well. His frame of mind had bounded up and down, back and forth. One moment he was on top of things, his people under his thumb, his authority unassailable. But the next moment would bring a wave of dark disorientation, as if things were not quite in sync, as if they were trundling along like some mad symphony played to two rhythms at once. He didn't like thinking about it. It only seemed to make things worse.

He had stayed up waiting for McKesson, working on a paper for the Institute's bi-monthly journal, but he couldn't get into it. Roth preyed on his mind. He had never liked Roth anyway. But lately he felt an almost consuming hatred for the man. It taxed him. He cursed Roth for it, only to find his hate level rise an additional notch.

By the time Lee brought the urn by to his room, Hoeksberg was more than ready to call it a day. His head ached in spite of the double dose of analgesic he had taken nearly a half hour before. He had accepted the artifact with little more than a grunt and plunked it in the corner of his room. Then he had gone to bed.

But he couldn't get to sleep. He knew it seemed crazy, but he couldn't get to sleep because of the urn.

It bothered him.

He turned toward the wall and lay there in the dark, feeling the thing over his shoulder. It was like the antique nutcracker his grandmother had given him as a boy. In the light it was toy soldier with a respectful countenance. But in the dark, the shadows played on the nutcracker's face, turning it into something that watched him out of the corners if its eyes and grinned threateningly. He finally got up and shoved the urn into his clothes closet. He slammed the door hard, checking twice to assure that it had clicked shut securely. He resolved to get rid of the thing in his next shipment of goods to the mainland.

Then he hit the mattress again. Sleep eventually claimed him, and the dream came almost immediately thereafter.

Hoeksberg was back in the office, seated in the darkness, facing the Shadowman. And the Shadowman was obviously displeased. He sat in silence, his black, faceless stare pinning Hoeksberg to the back of his seat like a bug in a mounting case. This time, Hoeksberg had no inclination to run. There was nowhere to run now, because he and the Shadowman were one. So Hoeksberg just sat, waiting. He felt a fat drop of sweat start at his armpit and tickle down over his ribs.

"We moved too slowly," the voice from the shadowface finally hissed. "We should have confiscated the urn immediately. We moved *far* too slowly. We must not make such an error again."

Hoeksberg had to swallow before he could speak. He shrugged very lightly, remembering the scannerbot.

"The mechanical device was already in operation. It was . . . in the way." The flimsiness of the excuse burned in his own ears. "But we have the urn now. And Roth will never get it back."

The Shadowman seemed unimpressed.

"We must send it away," he growled. "At the earliest possible convenience. And that is not all. We have more work to do now. Much more."

Hoeksberg winced at his tone, and the Shadowman continued. Sitting mutely and listening, at once revulsed and charmed, Hoeksberg soaked the words of the Shadowman into his soul like great droplets into an already swollen sponge. Still, the words sunk deeply, and in the final moments of the dream they brought back the first stirrings of that cold, powerful feeling he had drawn from the Shadowman before. Hoeksberg hungered for that feeling now. He craved it.

"You must be wary of the girl," the Shadowman warned finally. "Roth will try to contact her. He will have something, something that she needs. It is at the university now, and he is certain to discover it before long. Then he will attempt a communication. The girl is clearly an accomplice in his scheme."

Hoeksberg nodded. The fact was clear now, yes. The intimate little conversations in the lounge; the long hours spent together in the digiport bay, stretching late into the night. They had clearly been plotting together all along.

"She means to set us back, to sabotage our work. She has already done sufficient damage. She must be kept from plaguing us further, at all costs. If necessary, at the cost of her life."

Hoeksberg nodded once more. And smiled.

"There are forces out to destroy us, Roald. Silly, naive forces that fail to understand the scope of our might. We can beat them, you and me. The spoils will be ours for the taking. And our power will reign supreme, unchallenged."

Hoeksberg pondered the Shadowman's words, all of them. He savored them like rich wine. Victory would be sweet. Yes, very sweet indeed.

14

Roth stood before the secretary of the Zoology Department, up the hall from his new office in the Life Sciences Building, fuming. The new office was much smaller than his old one, tucked away in an obscure corner among some pressed vegetation and several years' accumulation of cobwebs. It was all the department had been able to scrape up for him on such short notice. And Roth understood that. The office didn't bother him at all.

The change in the SATCOM code did.

"I've been trying to reach Nordaustlandet on that number all morning. Since when has it been changed?" He did his best to keep his voice down. He knew it wasn't the secretary's fault.

She scanned a printout with her finger. "Just barely," she nodded. "The cancellation is dated today. Just barely this morning." She took a huge bite of a huge Danish. Both matched her figure.

He felt his shirt pocket for an Ionwriter and pulled out a scrap of paper to scribble on. "What's the replacement code?" he demanded.

The secretary just shook her head, cheeks bulging. "Classified with three stars. If you work in the president's office, you get access. Otherwise, forget it."

Roth stared at her incredulously.

"That code *can't* be classified! Nordaustlandet isn't a classified project, it never has been!"

The secretary just shrugged, licking a frosting-tacked crumb from her lower lip. She held up the print out.

"Says right here."

Roth clenched his fists. This was Hoeksberg's doing, he was certain of it. He had been trying to reach Lee on the SATCOM since seven o'clock, and the code just wouldn't go through. Now he knew why. It was just one more indication that Hoeksberg was doing his best to make good on his promise. There had been plenty of other signals already.

Almost from the time he had first arrived back at the university, Roth had been confronted by a maddening barrage of hassles. They were like the spit wads he and Ricky Mortimer used to peashoot at Mrs. Feeny back in Bickerton Elementary—they didn't cause any real damage, but they drove her absolutely bugbrains.

Now the shoe had shifted to the other foot, and it was Roth who was going bugbrains. Upon arrival, his first destination was Dean Wells's office. Roth was bound and determined to look Wells in the eye and make him either justify his signature on Hoeksberg's transfer document, or rescind it and send him back to the Corridors. Conveniently for the dean, he was indisposed. Hiding out, Roth surmised. And for good reason. Wells couldn't justify that signature, and Roth knew it. But he also knew that Wells didn't dare anger Hoeksberg, who had connections reaching clear up through the board of trustees.

One of those connections was Frank Mirisch, who in the meantime was supplying a whole new set of hassles.

His expedition was leaving for Brazil within ten days, and he required Roth's attendance at a myriad of upcoming briefings. He had already put Roth at the head of a team of four graduate students, all of whom were to spend the summer analyzing arrow toxins once used by local primitives. The assignment meant loads of paperwork—proposals, analyses, goal statements—all required prior to departure by the International Institute who was funding the project. There was no mention made of Roth's equipment, or the scanning process. Apparently the expedition didn't require them after all.

Of course, Roth itched to send Mirisch packing, to tell him that he had no intention of going to Brazil. But that would not have endeared him any further to the university administration, with whom he was already on shaky ground after his tangle with Hoeksberg. After all was said and done, Roth simply could not afford to jeopardize his position any further. His career aside, his affiliation with the university was his only link to the urn. Everything would come to a grinding halt if he lost his job. So now, all things considered, he found himself in the absurd position of trying to reach the dean so he could pull out of the expedition, while beginning frantic preparations for it at the same time.

To make matters worse—over and above all of the absurdity, the frustration, the chaos—Roth was growing worried. He had left Lee behind, a continent and a half away, fending for herself. There had been only one way for him to get in touch with her, and Hoeksberg had effectively squelched it.

Of course, there *was* one *other* way.

He looked up at the secretary again. The Danish was history. She was licking her fingers.

"I have some unfinished business back on the island," he declared resolutely. "Tell Mirisch I'm digiporting back for the afternoon. I'll be back first thing this evening." He turned and headed down the hall toward his office. If he hurried he might be able to leave within the hour.

Her voice stopped him short.

"I don't think so, Dr. Roth," she called in a warbling falsetto. When he turned back she was holding up a long, pink sheet. "Long distance digiport approval takes two weeks," she sighed. "Would you like to fill out a form?"

His eyes widened.

"Since *when* do you need *digiport approval*?"

She tipped her head and looked matronly. "Everybody and his graduate assistant is digiporting these days. Europe one minute, Asia the next. It all gets terribly expensive."

A heavy breath escaped through Roth's teeth. The secretary gave him a melancholy smile. "Besides," she reminded, "Dr. Mirisch has you scheduled for briefings most of the day." With that she handed him an agenda. He took twenty seconds to look it over.

They were the last free seconds he would have for nearly three days.

15

During those three days, as Roth sat trapped in unending meetings, Lee was wrestling with a decision. It was a decision that weighed on her with frightful heaviness, and yet there was no one on earth to whom she could turn for guidance.

She had tried to reach Roth at home at least a dozen times. She had called Frank Mirisch's office twice. The morning secretary had no idea where Roth was. The afternoon secretary had no idea *who* Roth was. Lee had even left a lengthy message on Roth's personal communication exchange at the university, telling him all about the discs and describing exactly what had happened during the scan.

No response. And time was slipping away.

Lee had peeked breathlessly into the main digiport bay every morning before breakfast, fully expecting to see a neat arrangement of sealed crates replacing Roth's clutter of scanner gear. So far her fears had not materialized. But it was only a matter of time. Hoeksberg had already shipped the urn to Oslo with Wong's last load of artifacts, Lee watching in helpless silence as it flickered into nothing out on the digiport pad. Now all she had left were the microdiscs. And whatever was encoded on them.

That was the big question. *What?* In three day's time, Lee had devised a lot of crazy answers to that question. But only one of those answers had demanded any real attention. It kept coming back, nagging, refusing to stay away. And it was the craziest answer of all.

The Lost Ten Tribes of Israel were on those discs.

Something inside her cackled with wild laughter at the very notion. It was straight off the cover of the International Enquirer, second only to the headline about the 92-year-old recluse that was eaten by killer cockroaches in Guatemala.

But something else inside her, something straight-faced and trembling just a little, wasn't laughing. It was asking *What if?*

What if, by some wild stretch of the imagination, it were true?

What if the Israelites captured so long ago by the Assyrians, carried away into the lands of the north, had managed to maintain a cohesive society? Like the children of Israel enslaved by Pharaoh. And what if, like the children of Israel, they had managed to engineer a mass exodus under divine guidance? Let's say they fled northward again, clear into the upper reaches of what centuries later would be called Scandinavia. And then, still pursued by their relentless overlords, they fled even further, into the frozen islands off the Norwegian coast. Into hiding.

Into the Corridors.

It was the same scenario that Lee had devised months ago, and had toyed with ever since.

Now that scenario had a sequel. It began with a runaway civilization struggling for survival against the arctic wasteland. Weeks grew into months, months into years, years into decades. And, like the desert wanderings of the children of Israel, the prolonged hardships eventually brought about a kind of purification among the refugees. But, unfortunately, for them there was no land of milk and honey waiting just over the horizon. Only endless glacial fields and excruciating cold. And, just a few decades away, impending extinction.

But extinction wasn't in the master plan. No, because according to scripture, the tribes would some day be brought back from the lands of the north to claim their rightful inheritance. So the plan had to include some means of preservation, some way to keep the tribes alive and well—for centuries upon centuries—until the time came for the fulfillment of ancient prophecy.

And now for the wild part.

What if that means of preservation worked like Roth's scanner? Except in reverse. What if, somehow, the dying tribes had been translated from living organisms into magnetic energy, and had been . . . well . . . *stored* somewhere. Somewhere safe and hidden, where they could rest unmolested, awaiting the day when they would be liberated once again?

Somewhere like the ten gold-plated iron rings imbedded in Roth's urn.

Ten rings.

Ten tribes.

Lee felt goosebumps tingle up her stomach and across her arms.

For three days she had reflected upon the idea, at first a little embarrassed to consider it with any seriousness at all. But the more she had meditated, the less uncomfortable she had felt. Finally she had gone to her knees, requesting a definite confirmation.

Had she received it?

Not really. Not yet. There was an answer though, of sorts, although it wasn't what she had wanted. She had felt it stirring inside, but she was afraid to let it out. It wasn't a yes, and it certainly wasn't a no. It was more like . . .

Try it and see.

She shuddered.

No thanks. I'm not really in a mood to experiment, and besides that, remember the rule about materializing live data? And besides *that* remember the way that Hoeksberg was looking at me the other night in the digiport bay, and remember what he could do to my project and my grades and my entire future if I deliberately went against one of his most adamant dictums? . . .

Try it. Run the data. Send it to the pad . . .

Huh-uh. No way. What if this is a mistake? What if I'm not hearing right, and all of this is really just coming from inside my own head, and I make some kind of horrendous mistake like Roth did with the monster, the woolly mammoth? . . .

Exercise your faith, Lee. It's right. Run it.

And the more she tried to argue, the more insistent it had become. Tonight it was becoming more insistent than ever. So she lay in the dark, wondering what Roth would do, dying for just thirty seconds with him over the SAT-COM. But there was no way, she knew. She couldn't reach him from her end because he was simply too hard to locate. And he couldn't reach her from his end because the Nordaustlandet communications code had been changed and classified. She had picked that little tidbit up from Wong during a chat in the lounge. She was as mystified about it as everyone else.

Lee, however, was not mystified. She still remembered the look on Hoeksberg's face, and Roth's warning.

She missed Roth more than ever.

She thought about him now, about the confidence he had placed in her. She thought about the scanner consoles, hypothetically boxed and waiting on the digiport pad, earmarked for American soil. She thought about Hoeksberg, about that night in the digiport bay, about what he could do to her if she crossed him.

She also thought about the woolly mammoth, and cringed.

She had been there with Roth the night he had materialized the thing. They both watched spellbound as the pad lit up, spit fire through its pores and gave birth to a blinding, quivering shape. She still remembered the look on Roth's face: jubilant, breathless, like a little boy who had finally figured out how to work a new toy and was in the process of trying it out. The materialization was nearly complete before they realized what it was going to produce. And by then it was too late.

It was the biggest thing Lee had ever seen. The mammoth towered over the pad, weaving ever so slightly, like a shaggy high-rise in the wake of a tremor. Then, with speed that was absolutely terrifying, it bolted.

Roth grabbed Lee, scrabbling out of the beast's path. With something between a howl and a roar it swept a massive tusk in their direction, missed and took out half of a digiport stabilization control. Lee still hadn't found her footing. Roth hurled her stumbling toward the door.

They flew out into the hallway. Behind them, the bay's massive double doors burst open and smacked their respective walls like oversized barroom louvers. The mammoth plowed through with a shrieking grunt. Head wagging, it attacked the red fire extinguisher case on the opposite wall like an enraged bull. On the other side of the wall, Wong and three students watched a pair of enormous ivory prongs punch through and rip back, opening a window onto something out of a nightmare. They exited with unparalleled haste.

Hoeksberg and Murray appeared at the opposite end of the hallway, in the doorway to the lounge, Hoeksberg yelling at the top of his lungs. The mammoth turned on them and charged. The pair climbed all over the top of each other in unabated panic. In the end, being larger, Murray got back into the lounge first.

Lee was too busy fleeing the chaos to witness the rest. Somehow Roth managed to locate one of the stunrifles the team used for protection during polar bear migration, and made it back to the lounge just as the mammoth crashed inside. He exhausted the weapon's main and auxiliary batteries bringing the animal down. It was subsequently dispatched by lethal injection and sent to the Institute for dissection. Fortunately, although the damages ran into the thousands, no one was injured. Except for Murray. Hoeksberg had given him a nasty scratch over the right eye trying to beat him out of the hallway.

But what if the whole thing happened again? Or something like it. Who knew *what* was on those discs. She certainly didn't. Not for sure anyway. What if she had misjudged things? What if she wasn't reading her feelings correctly? Maybe the inspiration she'd received was really no inspiration at all. Maybe all she was feeling was her own wild curiosity, mixed with a strong dose of conflicting apprehension. What if there was something un pleasant on those discs, just waiting to be unleashed? Something dangerous. Something deadly. Maybe . . . What if? . . .

As her mind poured over this long list of recollections, of doubts and terrible fears, Lee had edged slowly out of bed. She had pulled on her clothes and run an ineffectual brush through her hair. Then she had fished under the bunk, come up with the discs, and headed out the door toward the digiport bay. Because, all *maybe's* aside, there was really only one viable alternative. It was the same one Roth would have selected, had he been there.

Oh, how she wished he had.

16

Eight hours away from Nordaustlandet, a quiet work day was drawing to a close in the control room of the university communications complex. Ferdie Crump sat with his feet up on a panel of his relay board, eating pistachios and perusing the news as it scrolled with leisure over his central monitor screen. When the service line beeped he snatched up the receiver right from where he sat, never missing a word. He swallowed his mouthful and spoke.

"Central COM. Crump."

The voice on the other end of the line was not nearly so casual.

"Put me through to Cochran," it demanded curtly. The voice was ragged, mean.

Ferdie was unruffled. Most service calls were irate, so what? It was almost quitting time, and he was enjoying his pistachios.

"Cochran left at three-thirty. Whataya need?"

Nothing he could provide, he hoped. Ferdie could tell immediately that this guy was gonna be no real joy to work with. Let the big boss handle him tomorrow. Ferdie got paid for punching buttons. Cochran got the real bucks. He could take the flack, too. And from this guy there *was* going to be flack, it was already obvious.

"This is Roald Hoeksberg," the voice growled. "I'm calling over the Scandinavian exchange."

Ferdie's feet jerked reflexively from the relay panel. Pistachio shells exploded over his console. He cleared his throat.

"*Yes*sir. May I help you?"

Hoeksberg was nobody to play around with. He had friends, and he knew how to use them. Everybody knew that, particularly the boys at the COMMS complex. Hoeksberg had just finished muscling a code change through the system. It was a rush, and Cochran had balked at first. Shortly thereafter he had been called into the vice president's office for a "special briefing." He had come back looking like a whipped puppy.

"I ordered a code change three days ago. It hasn't gone through. I want to know why."

Ferdie's mouth hung open in a little round "o." His eyes flitted in confusion.

"Can you *hear* me out there?" the voice roared impatiently. "I thought you ran a *communications* operation!"

"Yes, sir," Ferdie shot back. "Perfectly well. Uh . . . there must be some mistake. The change was made, I'm sure of it. I entered that one myself." He knew suddenly that he shouldn't have admitted that. No, that hadn't been a good move at all.

"Then would you mind telling me, you lamebrained *moron*, why the president's office has received a down signal every time they've tried to get through? I called them just this morning, and they've been trying for three *days*!"

"Maybe there was an error on their printout," Ferdie offered humbly. He remembered the news on his screen and punched it away like a shot. A directory flashed in its place.

"You listen to me, you simpering fool. For your sake there had better not be an error, not in the printout, not in the data. Not anywhere."

Ferdie's fingers juggled over the keys, misspelling twice, finally entering the right command. Hoeksberg's name popped up, along with a long column of numbers. The guy had more phones than AT&T.

"Do you have any idea how much of my time you've wasted already?" the voice railed. "Do you have the slightest idea how much that time is *worth*?"

Ferdie's eyes were wide, pupils jumping. There it was, third from the top: the Scandinavian code he had just barely changed.

"I have it right here sir," he blurted. "On my screen."

"You have *what*?"

"The change. Made on the seventh, just like you ordered. Classified three-star."

"Wonderful," the voice answered bitterly. Then it grew into a rant. "So why haven't I been receiving my calls? *What are you people doing back there*?"

"I don't know . . . sir," Ferdie quavered, answering the first question before hearing the second.

"Your name," the voice demanded. "Give it to me. Now."

Oh, this was bad. This was really bad.

"Crump. Ferdinand Crump." A fake name. He should have given a fake name. Oh why, oh why hadn't he done that? His brain was stumbling like a dancer with one foot in a bucket.

"Listen to me, Crump, and listen well." The words were quiet, murderous. "I gave you every chance in the world. I even chose the *number* myself to make it easy for you. EL 46-5777-4942. Are you telling me your department can't even print out ten digits correctly!? *Ten simple . . .* "

Ferdie eyed the screen and did a double take.

"Sir," he cut in unevenly, "excuse me sir, but I see the

problem right here. There's been a mix up."

"Tell me something I don't know, idiot."

"We've just got the numbers switched, that's all." Ferdie's voice held tentative relief. "EL 46-5777-4942 isn't the replacement code at all. It shows here as your north campus lab extension."

The response fairly thundered. "*Can't you fools do anything right? I ask for one simple change, and you jumble my entire directory!*"

"But I didn't *touch* the rest of your . . . "

"If you haven't classified the number I requested, you maladroit half-wit, then what number *have* you classified? I'm trying to run a research project up here *without phone service!*"

"I show EL-24-1377-1155," Ferdie stuttered. "I'll arrange to have it switched for the other one first thing tomorrow morning . . . "

"You do nothing! *Nothing*! Just keep your incompetent hands off of my directory! I'll live with it as it stands. But you tell Cochran he'd better get his act together or he'll find himself on the *outside* of the next administrative shuffle. You understand?"

"Yessir."

The line died. Ferdie set down the receiver. Still shaking, he started picking pistachio shells off of his panel. He was almost finished before he realized that he had violated university policy.

He had given out a classified commcode without signature clearance.

* * *

Roth smiled through his exhaustion and penned the last few digits onto the scrap of paper next to his SATCOM. EL-24-1377-1155.

It hadn't been easy playing Hoeksberg. It had taken him nearly half an hour just to think up enough insults to guarantee intimidation. It had also cost him about eighty dollars to route his call out over the Scandinavian exchange and back through to the university. But it had been worth it. The new SATCOM code was his, and as soon as day began to dawn over Nordaustlandet (about 10:00 P.M. his time, he calculated) he would put it to good use and contact Lee.

Lee.

Despite the briefings, and the reports, and the unending paperwork, she had been on his mind almost constantly ever since his return to the States. Even now, his weary mind aching, nearly thirty-six straight hours without sleep, he still couldn't stop thinking about her.

He had managed to receive two of her messages. The second one had been the longer of the two, covering the details of the scan and the tidal wave of data recovered from the rings. (It neglected, however, to mention that Hoeksberg had commandeered the urn and shot it off to Oslo. That was something that Lee simply hadn't been able to disclose, not by message. She had been waiting to deliver that dismal tidbit in person.) This information was all very important to Roth. Obviously, he was still vitally concerned about the fate of the urn and the outcome of the scan. The sense of divine calling he had felt so strongly the night he reentered the caves still burned within him. But something else seemed to burn there as well. Lee was far away now, and Roth felt a loss that he had never known before. The strength of that loss had taken him completely by surprise. The feeling tugged at him. It wouldn't let up.

He wanted her back, pure and simple.

And he was worried. He just couldn't shake the inkling that some imminent peril lay in wait for her. The impression was vague, intangible. But it just kept coming back.

Checking his chronometer, Roth slumped heavily and rubbed at his eyes with his fingertips. He was late for another of Mirisch's great and glorious briefings. Thank goodness it was the day's last. He would attend it, doze where he could, and then return to his office and call Lee on the phone. That thought alone kept him going; it was the one bright star on his horizon. At ten o'clock he would hear her voice, and know that she was all right.

Between now and then, he could only pray that she actually was.

He got up, bumped into the door jamb, re-navigated, and headed for his next meeting.

17

Lee slipped along the main hallway toward the digiport bay, the foot-long microdisc box pulled tightly to her breast. Her heartbeat thrummed against it. The entire complex was now dimmed to night-level by the compound's twenty-four-hour lighting control module. She softly passed by the doors to several student quarters, all quiet as empty tombs. Around the corner, half way up the corridor, was the door to Hoeksberg's room.

A sliver of light beamed at the threshold.

Lee paused for a second, listening. No sound came from inside. Treading only on her toes, she edged to the far side of the hallway, away from the door. It was mostly dark now, not light and reassuring as it had been three nights before when she had delivered the urn. The memory of that night suddenly returned to her full force, and she saw Hoeksberg's face once more, floating evil and yellow in the blackness of the digiport bay. She didn't want to see that face again. Not here. Not in the dark, in a deserted hallway in the middle of the night, with no one else in sight.

She felt for the wall with her free hand, touched it and brushed back against it. But her eyes were on the door, on the slim white gap that pushed closer and closer with every step. She remembered the old 2-D vampire movie again, and although she tried to push the thought away, to banish it to the unpleasant, subconscious realm from which it had come, her mind could almost picture something lurking behind that door, just as it had lurked behind the cobwebs on the screen.

No. That's silly. Don't even think that, it's pointless and silly.

That something was dark and tall, cloaked and powerful, dead and cold. Cold and lilywhite and it grinned from the shadows with that familiar, hungry grin and when it touched you on the shoulder it was like ice. Oh, so cold you could feel it clear down in the marrow of your bones, and then it would start to squeeze and it would grin and it would squeeze

Stop it!

Only this monster wasn't lilywhite at all, was he Lee? No, he was yellow, a bright, sick yellow like the man in the moon, and he was right behind that door. Yes, she could picture him, black eyes wide and glaring like the eyes of something from an old 2D thriller, his ear at the jamb and his fingers wrapped around the knob waiting, just waiting for precisely the right moment, when Lee would be right across from the doorway and only a leap away, a single flying leap away

Please, stop it, please! . . .

She was there now, right across from the door, edging along the far wall like a hiker on a ledge. And it was getting colder. Maybe it was her imagination, but the closer she got to the door, the colder it seemed to . . .

A shadow split the crack of light.

The knob clinked and turned.

The microdiscs jumped in Lee's grasp. A scream leaped into her throat. She bit it back, her pulse crashing like surf in her ears. She would have spun shrieking and charged back down the hallway, but her legs were useless. They were dead, the legs of a rag doll.

The knob turned the other way, jiggled momentarily, and Lee heard the lock tumblers clack into place. Then the sliver of light under the door snapped to black.

Lee closed her eyes and fell silently against the wall, heaving giant, relieved lungsfull of noiseless air. As soon as her legs would carry her, she tottered from the doorway, crept around the corner, and headed for the entrance to the main digiport bay.

She was still shaking violently, rebuking herself for allowing her imagination to get so far away from her. That whole thing was stupid, she rated, senseless and stupid! She could have dropped the discs, she could have *screamed* for heaven's sake! Right in front of his door! And where would that have left her with all of her elaborate plans?

As she reproved herself, with every other step, she glanced back over her shoulder. The hallway remained mercifully empty behind her.

The security keypad next to the double doors glowed a faint green. Lee stepped in front of it and glanced back over her shoulder one final time. Her finger still trembly, she punched in the combination, a line of squarish, emerald numbers. Then she punched the UNLOCK key. The numbers blinked into letters:

ERROR.

Lee blinked back. She tried the combination again.

ERROR.

ERROR.

She gnawed her lip nervously. So, the SATCOM number wasn't the only code Hoeksberg had changed. He had beefed up security in the digiport bay as well. How grand. The entire compound was now safe for democracy.

Lee glanced both ways down the hallway. It would be so easy just to slip back to her room. There was no way she could get into the bay anyway. She certainly couldn't *break* through the door. It was tempered titanium alloy, built triple-strength to resist possible power overload on the pad. No way she could get in. Might just as well forget it.

But she couldn't.

How much longer would Roth's equipment remain there? The urn was out of reach, the discs were all she had left, and as soon as Hoeksberg shipped the scanner system off the island the discs would be useless. She had to act now, and she knew it. There could be no hesitation, not this late in the game.

All at once she had an idea. She glanced down toward the far end of the hallway. The door to the lounge hung half-open. Inside would be another door, and it would *not* be triple-strength, tempered titanium. It would be quite ordinary, secured only with an old-style, mechanical lock—the same kind that were installed in all of the doorknobs to all of their quarters. The very same kind, she remembered.

And that would be very convenient.

She made her way to the lounge and felt through the darkness until she found the entryway to the food prep area. Once inside she turned on the lights, sifted through the drawers, and found a pair of steak knives (which had yet to be used on anything more decent than syn-sirloin). They were identical to the knives she had used twice before when she had locked her keys in her room. Leaving food prep, she left the door just enough ajar to cast a thin glow about the main lounge area. On the other side of the area was the door to the secondary digiport bay.

Just as Lee had suspected, it was locked.

She stuck one of the knife blades between the door and the jamb. Both were old, and there was a generous gap. She slid the blade down toward the knob until in stopped against the door latch. Then she inserted the second blade and slid it up from underneath. Holding the blade tight against the latch, she twisted it to toward the knob.

The latch moved, she could feel it.

She held it in place with the top blade and twisted the bottom blade again, moving the latch further. And further. After a scant half-minute, the door clicked and swung open. A new record for Fingers McKesson.

She scooped up the discs, stepped inside, and closed the door behind her. Feeling along the wall for the touchpad, Lee switched on the room lights. A second touchpad on the digiport console brought it to life as well. Beside the touchpad was a dark red rectangle topping a miniature keyboard. The whole set of controls was labeled DESTINATION. Lee typed in the abbreviation and ID digits for the main digiport pad. They glowed in the rectangle. She beamed smugly. Popping open a black safety cover, she snapped three toggles, starting a ten-second countdown in a second rectangle. By the time it had reached "five," she was already standing at the center of the one-man digiporter.

She felt an odd warmth in her limbs which grew into a prickly sensation, as if her entire body had gone to sleep. The room fuzzed around her for just a second, then everything was white light. When the light faded, Lee found herself standing on a much larger pad behind the locked doors of the main digiport bay. Before her rested the scanner gear, ready and waiting.

She was in!

And now, all of the wild anxiety she had felt earlier in her room came flooding back unchecked.

* * *

Twenty-five minutes later Lee sat motionless, awash in the dim yellow glow of the computer terminal, her heart thudding. She had already logged on, typed in the code, slid the first disc into the drive and fed the data into the system. Now all that remained was to clone it, and send it to the pad.

She swallowed dryly.

Lee hit three keys, waited, hit two more. She winced at the quick series of beeps that preceded the cloning sequence. They blared like sirens in the night's silence, wailing through the cavernous digiport bay, echoing down the halls, calling to Hoeksberg. Almost certainly he would overhear them. Momentarily he would crash through the door and end everything in a fit of devilish fury.

Maybe it would be better to end it. End it now.

But the hallway remained silent.

Lee swallowed again. The cloning sequence was now complete.

Her fist backed toward her mouth and pressed against her lips. A gust of fear and misgiving whipped through her head like a dust devil. Just one key stared up at her from the keyboard, expressionless, inscrutable. It said, simply, SEND.

SEND.

The lady or the tiger?

SEND.

Try it, Lee. Run the data. Send it to the pad . . .

Without warning, her finger shot out. It hit the key hard enough to skid the board a good two inches and bonk it against the drive. The computer beeped and hummed. Lee shot a wide-eyed glance out at the pad.

And nothing happened.

The computer beeped again. Lee looked up at the terminal, watched for a few seconds, and her mouth dropped open. For several minutes she sat in suspended animation, incredulous. Then, even though she sensed deep inside that there was no mistake, she reloaded the data and tried again.

And again.

And she watched it happen one more time, the awe still deep in her eyes.

Now there could be no doubt, could there?

Lee ejected the microdisc from the machine and stared at it dully. Whatever it contained, it wasn't just raw genetic data. Oh, no. It was almost certainly some kind of program, and someone

(or Some One)

had to have written it. Because, three times in a row, it had swept the screen blank, had sent the cursor spitting across the screen to the upper left corner where it sat blinking patiently. Waiting.

For an access code.

Lee sat in the dark, pondering for what could have been an eternity, the cursor winking . . . winking . . . winking at her from the screen. We have a little secret, don't we?

At last she arose. Quickly and quietly she shut everything down. Then she padded breathlessly to the digiport console, initiated the countdown, and returned to the secondary bay in a shaft of light.

The door leading out to the lounge was still just slightly ajar. Stepping off the pad, Lee tiptoed to the crack and peered through to make sure the coast was clear. It was. She headed out across the lounge to the SATCOM station, where she would attempt to reach Roth for the fifteenth time. Wrapped snugly in her arms and nestled against her stomach, the carton of microdiscs clacked softly back and forth with each step.

And, at that very moment, Roth was discovering the key that would allow Lee to release the secret inside them.

18

The briefing ended at 8:15, and Roth had been back in his office before 8:30. Just an hour and a half to go, he had thought. He just had to last for ninety more minutes, and then he could call.

He had opened the window, visited the drinking fountain six times, paced off and on, and whistled. But finally, it was no use. He collapsed into his chair just to rest his legs for a minute, dropped his head onto his desk just to rest his . . .

Sleep claimed him almost at once.

Sometime later, from the depths of REM, came the dream.

* * *

It was night. Roth found himself on a hilltop. Far below, for miles and miles, cities sprawled aflame. Warriors milled, herding a weaving file of humanity toward the horizon. Toward the north. A thousand sounds ascended in the smoke, but the wailing was the worst. The worst by far.

Around him gathered a handful of old men—robed, bearded men with faces creased like dried fruit. All watched and listened in heavy silence. Prophets, Roth observed. Amos was there, as were Jeremiah and Daniel and Malachi. They seemed oddly familiar, like professional acquaintances made at some long-ago symposium. Roth realized almost immediately what they were witnessing.

"And I scattered them among the heathen," one of the old men brooded, "and they were dispersed through the countries."

Roth recognized the words. The old man was Ezekiel.

"Because they had despised my statutes, and polluted my sabbaths, and their eyes were after their fathers' idols."

Roth glanced at Ezekiel's face for just a second before flipping his gaze away again. The prophet was obviously not in the best of moods. No sense making eye contact with an irate seer.

Simultaneously, a hand touched his shoulder and a voice whispered in his ear: "And it shall come to pass in that day that the Lord will set his hand a second time to recover the remnant of his people. And the ransomed of the Lord shall return."

The passage was from the Old Testament. But the voice was from the caves at Nordaustlandet. It was the voice that had saved his life.

Roth turned. The eyes meeting his were kind, expectant, the eyes of a friend. It was the old man from the first dream. It was also, Roth knew now, the prophet Isaiah.

"And soon it *will* come to pass," Isaiah nodded. "Will it not?"

Roth just nodded back silently. He was certainly in no position to disagree. Apparently noting some uncertainty, the prophet raised his eyebrows. The others were turning now too, interested.

"Thou *hast* fetched the urn? . . . "

"Yes," Roth answered, now feeling vaguely on the hot seat. "It's . . . it's still at the compound."

"Good," Isaiah beamed. "Thine errand will soon be fulfilled, I trust." And before Roth could respond, the prophet turned, gazing out and down. Firelight glistened in his eyes.

"God's chosen are not lost, my brethren," he declared reverently. "They gather on paths of iron, before the gate of time. Ten paths, and one gate, locked tight by the Lord of Hosts. And so they stand, and wait. They wait for a servant, with the key."

All at once, in his dream, Lee's second message flowed back from his memory and Roth knew. Yes, it was very clear. Once they had waited on ten paths of iron. But not any more. Now they were gathered on forty-seven microdiscs full of live data. And they waited . . . for a servant with a key?

What *key*?

"The key?" Roth asked. "Where is the key? *What* is the key?"

His eyes never leaving the sky, the prophet pointed. Just above the horizon, one bright star shone from the handle of what Roth recognized immediately as the Little Dipper. It was Polaris. The North Star.

Isaiah turned abruptly to another of his colleagues.

"Thou hast the key, Brother Daniel?"

Daniel turned to Roth, who did a double-take. Because this Daniel had never even been close to a lion's den. It was Dan Miles, who taught astronomy back at the university. He and Roth had started the same year. Dan nodded knowingly at Roth.

"I have it, yes. It's in my lab, in the Physical Sciences Building."

"You have what?" Roth demanded, now hopelessly confused. "The North Star? What? . . . "

"I have the key." Dan repeated calmly. "To the Millennium File."

Then, from somewhere in the distance, came the buzzing of a pictophone. And Roth was back in his apartment, groping for the receiver.

19

Lee was flabbergasted that she had actually located Roth at his office. At first the voice on the other end of the connection sounded like it belonged to someone else. It was thick and slurred, a voice roused from deep sleep.

"Dr. Roth," she asked doubtfully, "is that you?"

"Yeah…" he answered. She could tell now that it really was him. But he sounded foggy, disoriented.

"Yeah… It's me…"

"It's Lee. Are you all right?"

He came out of the stupor like a shot.

"*Lee?*…Lee how are you? My heaven it's good to hear your voice!"

She felt exactly the same way.

"It's good to hear yours too. I'm fine, just fine." And hearing him Lee did feel fine. She felt finer than she had in ages.

"It's been a madhouse here," Roth was saying. "I tried to call up there but Hoeksberg changed the code."

"I know. Nobody can call in…"

"Well, I can now," he interrupted. "I got hold of the number this afternoon. I was waiting till tomorrow morning, though. I didn't want to call in the middle of the night. Figured it might cause more problems than it would solve." Only the barest trace of fogginess was left in his voice now.

"I got all your messages. How is everything? What's happening?"

She took a breath. She didn't want to tell him, but, of course, she would have to sooner or later anyway.

"The urn's gone. Hoeksberg got it. He sent it to Oslo three days ago." She could imagine his face, contorted in shock, so she hurried on before heart failure had a chance to set in. "But I don't think it matters. We have the discs, you got my message about the discs?…"

There was a moment of silence from Roth's end of the connection.

"Dr. Roth?" she ventured. Suddenly she felt awkward calling him that. There was so much between them now.

Yet she had never called him anything else. "Dr. Roth is everything?..."

"It's all right, yes. At least I think it is." She could envision him cogitating. From five thousand miles away she could almost hear the gears turning in his head. "Yes," he repeated finally, "the discs are all we need. They must be." He thought for a moment more and then his voice came again, dropped nearly to a whisper.

"Have you tried running them?"

"Yes!" she cried, abruptly re-remembering why she had tried calling him again in the first place. "Just tonight, I just barely finished. But they wouldn't run. I tried three times..."

Roth broke in, cutting her off.

"What's wrong... some kind of glitch?" His alarm was readily apparent, so she raced on to avert another potential coronary. "No, no glitch. It's the data. This sounds really wild, but it's not *just* raw data. It's some kind of program. When I tried to send it to the pad, it demanded an access code. Like a protected file. I couldn't believe it!"

There was another short pause at the other end of the line. Then there was laughter. It was weary, but it was bright and full at the same time.

"*That's* what he meant!" Roth exclaimed. "That's the key! The *access code*!"

"What key?"

"I had another dream, Lee, just before you called. I think I know what the access code is."

Lee's mouth hung open. "You do?"

There was wonder in his voice. "I think it's here. Right here at the university. As crazy as it seems, I think I was *supposed* to be sent back here. It all must be part of the plan."

She listened to him without the slightest idea of what he was talking about. But she didn't care. It sounded like the answer to everything, and it sounded just marvelous.

"I can get it tomorrow morning," he said. "About... five in the evening, your time. You can take the SATCOM into the digiport bay and hook into the automodem. I'll send the code straight into the computer over the phone. Everybody will be up and around, though. Can you manage that?"

"I'll find a way to manage it," she said, wondering how in the world she was actually going to do it.

"Whatever you do," Roth warned, "don't let Hoeksberg find out what's going on. He'll throw a wrench into things, I'm sure of it. I think he's..." Then he stopped, and Lee heard a short, indecisive breath. She knew what he was thinking, what he was reluctant to say. She finished the sentence for him.

"That he's on the other team. That he's in league with the devil."

She felt a shudder when she said it. Underneath, she had already suspected. But she had been afraid to acknowledge her fears.

"You think he is?" Roth asked.

"Do you?"

Another pause.

"There *was* something about him, that night in his quarters. I told you about it."

She nodded. "It's worse now. It's like..." Her voice cracked just a little. She didn't know how to finish. She thought of his sneer, his grip, the terrible cold hovering just outside his office door.

"Oh, Lee," Roth sighed, "I wish I could be there with you. I feel like I've put you through so much, and I've worried about you for days. Are you up to this? Can you pull this all together?"

Her heart was pounding. It was pounding because of the fear, because of what she knew she had to do. And it was pounding because of what she heard in Roth's voice. For her.

"I'll be okay."

"I love you, Lee."

She started. The words came so fast, so unexpectedly that it took a second for her feelings to catch up with them. Then tears filled her eyes.

"I love you too."

"I want to see you... we need to talk. When this is all over I'll fenagle digiport clearance somehow and I'll come up there, I promise. You know, we'll do some swimming, lay out on the beach, wiggle our toes in the hoarfrost."

She laughed and sniffed. "Get a freezer burn..."

They laughed together for a moment. The she grew serious again.

"In the meantime, you pray for me, okay? I think I'm gonna need all the help I can get."

"I already have. You do the same for me, huh?"

She nodded.

"You just take good care of yourself tomorrow. Be careful. *Really* careful." The deep concern in his voice was easy to read. It warmed and chilled her at the same time.

"I'll stay low profile, don't worry," she said. And then she thought of something. She had nearly forgotten it in the heat of the moment.

"D... Derek." She'd almost called him "doctor" again. "Tell me something. One last thing before we have to go." She already knew the answer to this question, but she needed to hear it now from him, point blank. It seemed amazing that, even up until now, they had never discussed it specifically.

"What's on those discs?" she asked. "What's going to come up on the pad when we send it through?" Her voice had distilled down to nearly nothing. "It's... it's the Lost Tribes, isn't it? The Lost Tribes of Israel."

There was no hesitation, no doubt.

"That's right, Lee," Roth said, his voice tired but strong. "And tomorrow we're going to bring them back. The two of us."

She nodded quietly. Then they just sat there for a while, together, separated by half a hemisphere, sharing the moment in awesome silence.

* * *

At the same time, in a darkened room on the other side of the compound, Roald Hoeksberg sat and brooded, his mind roiling black and cold like water under Arctic ice. A SATCOM receiver was propped against his ear, tuned to the same frequency as the receiver in the lounge.

He had heard everything.

III
The Final Standoff

20

Lee knew something was going to go wrong the moment she woke up the next morning. She tried to shrug the feeling off but it hung on stubbornly, like a cat over water. Something was in the air. She could feel it.

By eleven the wind tapered off and allowed the temperature to rise for the first time since Roth's clandestine trip into the caves. The pad operable, Hoeksberg ordered his crew out to the Corridors again. Lee now plowed silently through the snow toward the digs. She cursed the cold, she cursed the thigh-deep snow, she cursed her ever-bagging and ever-awkward Thermofoams. She was grumpy, on edge, and this asinine trip out to the work site wasn't helping any. It didn't make any sense anyway. She glanced toward the south where another scowling cloud bank was already building. A south wind hissed against her snow shields. Chances were, a new storm would be upon them within an hour. And then, before they had been able to accomplish anything even remotely worthwhile, they would all be hustled back to the compound again. Wong had tried to tell that to Hoeksberg. Lee had overheard them in the lounge. But Hoeksberg wouldn't listen to her. Hoeksberg never listened to anybody.

Where *was* Hoeksberg, anyway?

Lee stopped right there in the snow. Up ahead, Wong was blazing a faint gray trench through the whiteness. Four students followed in her wake. Just four. Two were missing.

Lee glanced behind her at the pad, which sat in the middle of the shallow snow-crater they had melted as they had digiported out. The pad was still and cold and lifeless now. No one else was coming.

The feeling of foreboding Lee had battled all morning tightened its grip on her heart.

Go back Lee. Go back to the compound.

She turned back to Wong, who plodded onward, like a fat gray duck leading four elephantine ducklings. They were almost to the entry now. None of them glanced back at her.

You don't have much time, Lee. Get back there now.

She took a halting step backward. Then she turned on her heel and ran. Sliding onto the pad, she pulled off a glove and began punching coordinates into the destination window on the small, adjoining control panel. Abruptly she stopped. Maybe it was just a hunch, but she somehow felt it inadvisable to materialize on the main pad. She canceled the digits and started over.

779.02

It was the ID code for the secondary pad, off the lounge. She hit the activator switch and waited for the electronics to count down.

* * *

Lee materialized and stepped into the empty lounge, shedding her foams as she walked. She tossed her snow shields onto one of the tables, padded softly to the doorway and peered down the adjoining hall. She was greeted only by heavy silence.

THE FINAL STANDOFF

No. No there was something. From up ahead, where the hallway turned a corner, a faint murmur echoed, rising and falling in a conversational cadence.

Lee stepped through the door. Her first two footfalls clacked solidly on the duraplex flooring. She shed her shoes, slid them to the wall with the side of a foot and tiptoed from there. The cadence became louder, more familiar. Lee's heart ticked in her throat.

She turned the corner. Twenty yards up the hall, the double doors to the digiport bay hung wide open. Two of the voices reverberating from inside were now readily identifiable. One was Hoeksberg's, the other was Murray's. The third was still muffled and faraway. Nevertheless, before Lee ever slipped to the door and peeked around the corner, she knew precisely what they were up to. The realization pumped a super-economy-sized jolt of adrenaline into her chest.

One quick glance confirmed all her fears.

Wires trailed everywhere. One of the mainframes was on its side; Murray was at work on another. Hoeksberg was crouched at the back of Roth's main drive unit, hands toiling furiously. And he was talking about Broger, that was the worst of it. Niles Broger was one of Hoeksberg's cronies at the University of Oslo.

All the color dropped out of Lee's face. This was it. They were finally packing up the gear for shipping. But they weren't sending it back to Roth in the states. Not if what she had just heard was any indication. No, they were sending it to Oslo. And from there, there was no telling what might happen to it.

For a single horrified second Lee didn't have the slightest idea what to do. Then light dawned in her eyes. She turned and rushed away toward her room.

21

Hoeksberg jerked two color-coded plugs out of the back of Roth's primary drive unit, unravelled some wires and started in on the screws to the main connecting cable.

"But can you *do* that?" Murray asked. He held one of Roth's mainframes on a tilt while another student worked on something up underneath. "All this stuff is Roth's, isn't it?"

Murray wasn't averse to following instructions, but there was something about this that just didn't feel quite right. Maybe it was simply the fact that he was working side by side with Hoeksberg. That sounded strange, he knew, but lately he'd been getting some wierd vibes from the guy. Of course, he'd never really been Murray's favorite person in the world. But for the last two days he'd been especially hard to live with. And not only that. There was a feeling about him—a creepy feeling like the guy was, well, bad. Not just bad like your typical, hard-nosed, cut-throat university bureaucrat. No, Hoeksberg had always been like that. This bad was *really* bad. Malicious. Maybe even downright evil.

Hoeksberg answered flatly, his eyes on his work. "Every piece of this equipment was purchased with university funds, Mr. Hale. Every single piece." He changed tools, grunting a little as he spoke. "And Dr. Roth certainly won't be needing any of it where he's going. This is little more than a prototype anyway. We might just as well send it to Broger and let him take a look at it."

"So what's he gonna do with it?" Murray pressed. "Roth's the only one who knows how it works." He let the mainframe creep too close to the floor. Muffled objections echoed from underneath. He tipped it back up again.

Hoeksberg peered at him from around the corner of the drive unit, looking right into his eyes. And, for no good reason, the hair prickled at the back of Murray's neck.

Crazy, wasn't it? How your mind started fizzing out after being cramped up in the same bunch of buildings with nine other people for eight months. There were days that Murray had wanted out before, days when he would have given anything to be back in the sunshine, kicking around barefoot with a girl on his arm. No, two girls. But today he wanted out like he had never wanted out in his life. He wanted away from Hoeksberg. About a hundred miles away. Maybe another planet.

"My dear Mr. Hale," Hoeksberg began. There was nothing dear in his voice whatsoever. "By the time Broger finishes dissecting this monstrosity he'll no doubt have devised improvements that Roth never even considered. Then we can all send it back to the inventor with our compliments." He raised his eyebrows dryly. From beneath them his eyes shone with a menacing luster. "Are you sufficiently satisfied with that response, or would you care to question my judgement further?"

Hoeksberg's eyes were still riveted on Murray, who swallowed hard. This was it. This was going to be his last semester. At the end of the term ol' Murray was taking off for the sunshine and the girls and he was taking off for good.

Hoeksberg glanced toward the floor and motioned casually to the mainframe with his clamptool. "You're crushing Mr. Winfield again..."

There were more muffled cries. Murray tipped back again. For the next several minutes he kept a close eye on Winfield. Murray wasn't just being cautious. He had no desire to look over at Hoeksberg again.

Silence overtook the room, broken only by the tiny clicks and taps of busy hand tools. Then a voice came from the doorway.

"Put your tools down and get away from the equipment."

Standing closest to the doorway, Murray glanced up. Lee stood just inside the bay, her chest heaving. In one hand she held the SATCOM and a container of microdiscs. In the other was one of the compound's stunrifles. It was leveled squarely at Murray's chest. His stomach flopped over.

Yep, he told himself, this was *definitely* his last semester.

* * *

Lee's pulse rocked in her chest, quivering the stunrifle barrel in quick, convulsive beats. There was no turning back now. She had gone to Plan Z, the last resort. From here on out it was do or die.

"Miss McKesson," Hoeksberg said, standing slowly. "What on earth are you doing?" His voice was cool and controlled.

The barrel swept toward him. Lee had seen this kind of thing in videoholos and old 2-D's, and it always looked tough and fairly exciting. Lee, however did not feel either tough or excited. She felt like she was going to wet her pants.

"If you don't get away from that equipment right now," she quavered, "I'm going to shoot you."

Hoeksberg's eyebrows lifted, but his eyes showed no surprise. They were dead eyes, gray and haunted. Murray glanced at him tensely.

"She's crashed a disc," he said. "Bugged out."

Bewildered, Winfield finally pulled his head and shoulders out from under the mainframe to see what was happening. It was a good thing.

"What's goin' on?" he asked.

Lee's tension finally erupted full force. "*I said get away from it!*" she screamed. "*All of you!*" She swung the gun at Murray again. He jumped back and the mainframe banged to the floor. Winfield swore and jerked his hand away.

"Okay, okay!" Murray yelled back, raising his hands like a holdup victim in a bad western.

"You too!" she shouted at Winfield. He scrambled to his feet. She jerked the barrel toward Hoeksberg. "Move!"

They backed slowly toward the door. She moved along, covering them. Things were feeling a little more movie-ish now. She had the upper hand, no question about it. Nevertheless, she kept a tight eye on Hoeksberg. He stared back at her wickedly as she set the discs and SATCOM on the floor.

"What are you trying to accomplish, Miss McKesson?" His eyes were narrow, shrew eyes. "Are you trying to save this equipment for Dr. Roth?" She continued edging them back, tight-lipped. "Because if you are you are wasting your effort. All of this will be shipped back in due time. Didn't you know that? Dr. Roth has nothing to worry about." Hoeksberg spoke softly, like a man extending a piece of candy with one hand and concealing a knife behind his back with the other. The lie was unbelievably obvious. Bristling, Lee backed him through the door and out into the hallway, pushing Murray and Winfield along behind him. They spread three abreast outside the threshold.

"You, on the other hand, may have reason to be concerned," Hoeksberg continued, his voice roughening. "Because if you continue this behavior, you will most certainly be expelled from the university. And you may be the target of legal action as well."

"Shut up," she snapped. The words felt hollow. She slid her hand up the door, toward the handle.

"Do you have any idea what I could do to you, Miss McKesson?" Hoeksberg was growling now. "Do you understand the depth of my power? I could destroy you. I could make a wasteland of your entire career... your entire *life*." Murray was eyeing him with quiet incredulity, his mouth half-open.

"Back off, against the wall," Lee demanded. She glared at Hoeksberg with all the gutsiness she could muster and motioned across the hallway with her weapon. "Back off, all of y..."

Winfield's hand suddenly shot out and snapped at the rifle barrel. He snagged it loosely and ripped it from Lee's grasp. Losing his hold, he grappled in vain after the weapon, finally knocking it clattering down the hallway. Lee stared after it, wide-eyed.

There was a moment of shocked inaction.

Then everybody lunged. Hoeksberg was first. Murray was right at his back. Winfield, still half-way after the rifle, came in a poor third. They all crashed against the door which Lee had already swung to within a foot and a half of closing. She saw immediately that she had moved too late. It would never have a chance to click shut.

But she had forgotten to take mass into account. Groaning on its hinges, the door bulldozed in slow motion, carrying the three frantic men right along with it. Then it clicked casually into its latch. Lee pushed a button and threw the emergency electro-bolt. She fell against the door, panting hoarsely, and smiled in weak relief. The bolt could only be re-opened from inside.

Out in the hall she could hear Hoeksberg raging. He screamed something... something about cutting their way into the bay. Murray's voice returned another something that sounded like an objection. Hoeksberg yelled again, louder. Lee was still smiling. She had a good idea what Murray was saying. They simply didn't have anything that would allow them to break through a triple-walled, tempered titanium door. Not within hours, anyway.

She brushed her hair out of her eyes and took a look at her chronometer. It was scarcely noon. Roth was five hours away with the code. She skimmed the bay for other means of entrance. The dim outline of another double-door met her gaze on the other side of the room. It was a cargo door, leading outside. Lee sprinted to it, throwing another electro-bolt.

Then she remembered the secondary digiport bay.

She ran back to the main console, flipped two switches, and watched the controls light up. Then she reached back behind the unit and opened a small compartment to reveal a bank of chips. She listened as the door to the compartment rose. A microswitch clicked audibly into position. She checked the countdown window. It flashed the word MAINTENANCE, and she smiled with satisfaction. As long as the rear compartment remained open, the unit thought it was being repaired and would accept no incoming beams. For the time being anyway, Lee was safe from intrusion.

She stepped to the scanner gear and gave it a once over. Most of the components were already dismantled, all of the plugs and fittings coded either by color or shape. Roth had shown her how it all fit together more than once, and she had helped with repairs on three separate occasions. It would be a tough job getting it all back together. But after all, she had five hours to kill.

Five hours.

She glanced back uneasily at the door. It was triple-strength, she reminded herself. Tempered titanium alloy. There was no way that Hoeksberg or anybody else could get through it in just five hours. No way in the world.

She hoped.

22

Roth stood in the east wing of the Physical Sciences Building, drumming his fingers nervously against a door. The nameplate on that door said DAN MILES. Underneath, in smaller letters it said SPECTROGRAPHY LAB. Underneath that, hand-scraped into the wood in even smaller letters, it said UNDERGRADUATE TORTURE CHAMBER. Dan had rubbed ink into the letters to make them stand out. Among the phy sci students, Dan's exams were both infamous and legendary, and he was proud of them.

Roth drummed his fingers some more. Behind the door was an open lab with two dozen or so work stations. On the other side of the lab would be a pair of cavernous storerooms. If Roth remembered right, three walls of the larger room were lined with a complex of small, locked drawers. Inside one of those drawers was the key to the Millennium File. Roth was certain of it.

He checked his chronometer. It was 9:15 A.M. That made it 5:15 P.M. in Nordaustlandet. He was already fifteen minutes late getting back to Lee, and there was no sign of Dan Miles. Which was odd, because Miles had a reputation for punctuality.

Roth checked his chronometer again. It was now 9:*16* A.M. If it got much later, he would try calling Dan at home. He didn't want to, because he wanted his whole approach to appear extremely casual. For the same reason, he hadn't walked over to the department office to ask when Dan would be in. He didn't want to call the slightest attention to himself, raise a single hair of a single administrative eyebrow. He couldn't afford to take any chances.

Hoeksberg had too many friends, and word traveled fast along the bureaucratic grapevine. Roth needed a favor from the Physical Sciences Department, and the best way to guarantee hassle-free delivery would be to keep it between buddies. Just Dan and him.

It was now 9:18. And counting.

All at once the door opened, butting Roth solidly in the tailbone. A pair of bleary, undergrad eyes peeked out into the hallway.

"Sorry, man. Didn't know you were there."

Roth rubbed his seat.

"That's quite all right." His voice groaned lightly. "I'm looking for Dr. Miles. Do you know where he might be?"

The student ran a hand over his face. He needed a shave. When he spoke, Roth sidestepped the breathblast.

"You got me," the undergrad shrugged. "I been in there studyin' most of the night. My lights finally blew out about five this morning. Been sleepin' like a baby."

Roth now understood why no one had answered the door.

"I got three big exams and two papers due over the next four days. More comin' after that. Lemme tell ya', finals are a real kick in the teeth."

Roth wished the student had taken the opportunity to brush his teeth before initiating the conversation.

"Do you have any idea when Dr. Miles will be in?" Roth asked.

"You got me," the student repeated. "He's got a class at..." And then the student's eyes cleared. Not much, but enough. He turned to Roth, who sidestepped again reflexively.

"No... we don't have class today. Miles is outta town."

Roth's pulse stepped up to double-time.

"He's *what*?"

The student nodded. "Outta town. Went to some kind of convention or somethin'. He told the class about it, but

I can't remember what he said, you know?"

Roth's pulse hit double double-time.

"When's he coming back?"

"You got me," the student said for what Roth suspected must have been the hundredth time. "Class meets again next Monday." He scanned the hallway for a clock. "What time you got anyway?"

Roth looked dully at his chronometer again. His mind was scrambling a-mile-a-minute in another direction.

"Uh... nine-twenty."

"Oh, listen, I'm late for cryogenics." The student took off at a trot. "Catch you later!"

Roth stood in the bare hallway and stared after him. In his head, he heard the seconds ticking steadily away.

23

The pounding started at one-thirty. It took Lee off guard, and she jumped hard enough to bend a connector pin on the scanner monitor's second port. Fortunately, she was able to bend it back without even breaking a fingernail. After that she worked more carefully. It took her a good four and a half hours to assemble it all—the mainframes, the scanner drive, the grid, the scannerbot and all of the attendant interfacing—and the pounding provided a constant accompaniment. It resonated through the bay's empty shell like the booming of a giant drum.

Now it was after six, and the pounding went on.

Lee sat in the tattered chair that formed a matching set with Roth's old scanner monitor and keyboard. The SAT-COM rested in her lap. It should have beeped over an hour ago, but it hadn't. And despite her best efforts, she was getting scared.

She had started out okay, perhaps because there had been plenty to do. But once the computer gear was reassembled, the situation had toughened up in a hurry. Like Peter on the waters of Galilee, she found her faith beginning to thin out as time wore on, allowing her to sink. She had started what-ifing again—What if Roth couldn't get the code? What if all the communication channels were tied up? What if Roth had some kind of accident?—and had finally forced her brain's worry-center to shut up by running some scanner tests. Pulling one of Roth's old discs she had materialized some Arctic cottongrass and three species of blue-green algae. They all came up clean as a whistle, and so she surmised (what did she know?) that she had managed to connect everything in proper order. Next she loaded the data from all forty-seven of the urn discs. Then she cloned the data and tried running it. Once again, it demanded an access code. Everything was set to go.

All that was left after that was waiting. And waiting, she found, was not her favorite pastime. In fact, it was making her faith thin out again like nobody's business. She was already up to her neck in the jitters and sinking deeper with each passing minute. No, the waiting was definitely doing nothing for her positive mental attitude. The pounding wasn't helping either.

The pounding. That went on. And on. And on.

She stared at the double door leading out into the hall. A slight ripple had already begun to form alongside the left hinges. Lee couldn't imagine what they were hitting the wall with. Certainly, no type of hand tool had even the slightest chance of inflicting any real damage. It was utterly absurd. An exercise in absolute futility.

So why were they still at it? Why hadn't they given up hours ago?

The jitters were lapping up over her chin when the SAT-COM beeped in her lap and very nearly gave her heart failure. She grabbed up the receiver, juggling it like a tryout for P.T. Barnum.

"Derek!"

"Lee... Sorry I'm late getting to you. I ran into some trouble."

"*You* ran into some trouble!..."

His voice was instantly on guard. "What's happened? You all right?"

Lee rubbed here eyes with her fingertips. She was starting to get a headache. "I caught Hoeksberg trying to pack up the gear and ship it to the mainland. So I got a stunrifle and forced him out of the main bay at gunpoint."

"You *didn't.*" Roth's delight was undisguised. She could tell he was proud of her. Somehow it was irritating.

"There wasn't much else I could do," she continued. "That was around noon. Now I'm holed up in here. It's cold, I'm thirsty, Hoeksberg and Murray and everybody else is trying to beat the door down, and I have to go to the bathroom. What took you so long?"

He took a deep breath.

"Dan Miles is the man I have to see here. Right now he happens to be away at a convention. I talked with one of his st..."

"What convention?" Lee demanded. "You mean he's *out of town?*"

"Don't panic. Let me finish. I talked with one of his students. Miles is in San Francisco. I thought at first he might be gone till next week, but his secretary says he has to be back by tomorrow morning for a guest lecture."

"Tomorrow morning... *your* time," Lee said.

"Right. Tomorrow evening, yours."

She let out an interminable sigh.

"I'm sorry, Lee. I don't know what else to do. Can you hang in there till then?"

Despite Roth's upbeat tone, the concern in his voice was now intense; Lee could feel it.

"I better," she returned. "If Hoeksberg gets hold of me, he'll kill me." She had intended that as a dry exaggeration. But the words came out with a tone of dreadful validity she didn't like at all.

"I'm on my way over to set up the modem," Roth told her, "but I'll call you back every couple of hours, on the nose. Okay babe?"

She nodded heavily. "I wish I could see you."

"Same here. I love you."

"I love you too."

"Keep the faith."

"Same to you."

The pounding rolled on, swelling to fill her ears again as soon as Roth's voice faded into the receiver. She started missing him passionately just as soon as she hung up. As if in response to her unspoken yearning, the SATCOM beeped again.

"Derek?..."

Her voice caught in her throat. There was a low, breathy laugh on the other end of the connection.

"No, Miss McKesson. I'm afraid not." The voice rang with dark glee. It was ugly, maniacal. "There is something happening outside your door, Miss McKesson. Do you hear it?"

A shiver snaked up Lee's back.

"I'm coming in to get you, Miss McKesson. And there's nothing you can do to stop me. Not you or anyone else."

Lee shuddered. The voice in her ear was revolting and she wanted it out, she wanted it gone. But her hand was cemented around the receiver like a chunk of ice. She couldn't lower it.

"I heard your little talk. Your little tete-a-tete with your darling Mr. Roth. Very sweet, I must say. But he will never get back to you in time, Miss McKesson. Never. *Never.*"

The voice was Hoeksberg's. And yet it wasn't Hoeksberg's. It was the voice of a medieval torturemaster, hooded in black, standing before an iron maiden.

"When I get through that door, do you know what I'm going do? I'm going to destroy every vestige of that equipment. I'm going to shatter your little plan into a million pieces. No one plots against me, Miss McKesson. *No one!* Quite shortly you will be so, so sorry that you ever allied yourself with Mr. Derek Roth. More sorry than you can imagine. Do you *understand me?*"

Lee's breath was a whine. She shook from somewhere deep inside. Mercifully, her hand was starting to thaw, to drag the receiver down from her ear.

"I'm going to hurt you, Miss McKesson," Hoeksberg hissed, his voice rising to a crescendo. "I'm going to hurt you very, very badly. And if I have the opportunity, I'm going to k..."

The receiver crashed down onto the SATCOM cradle. Lee allowed a single, terse sob to escape her throat and pressed her face into trembling hands. Still the pounding went on and on, and suddenly she could take no more, she was going to scream against it, scream at the top of her lungs until they stopped until they had to stop!...

No.

With supreme effort she swallowed the scream and breathed. She could not afford to let him do this to her. She had an entire night and most of a day ahead of her, and if she allowed herself to lose it now she was as good as gone. She would be giving up. And she couldn't do that. Her task was much too important for that.

She forced her hands into her lap, pressed her eyes shut and drew a long, slow draught of cold air into her lungs.

She let it out and drew another, then another, until the shakes began to subside.

Then, for the next few hours, she prayed.

24

The pounding stopped at approximately 8:30 P.M.

Lee went to her knees again in thanksgiving. The quiet was heavenly, and she let it flow over her like a balm. The only sound invading the stillness now was the baleful song of the wind outside, baying over the contours of the eaves and walls. There was an occasional rat-a-tat of ice flakes too. But those sounds were blissful by comparison. Perhaps Hoeksberg and his muscle-men had finally given up. More likely, they were only taking a break. But right now it didn't matter. Right now it was ecstasy.

The silence was still uninterrupted at nine o'clock when Roth checked in with his final call of the night. Lee was exhausted by then, and beginning to feel like she might be able to get some sleep. Roth agreed to check back with her first thing in the morning. They exchanged a long good-bye, full of the quiet, tentative intimacies often shared by new lovers discovering new feelings. By the time she hung up the SATCOM, Lee was enjoying a blend of peace and euphoria she would have thought impossible only an hour earlier.

Lee's last matter of business before she retired was to locate some additional clothing. The air was brutally cold. She had begun feeling it more than an hour before, and now she could clearly see her breath. Hoeksberg had apparently shut off the heat. He undoubtedly would have shut off the electricity as well, if the digiport bay hadn't been tied directly into the main supply. Lee knew that the bay also had an auxiliary generator for emergency power:

it would never do to lose electricity with some unfortunate research team or another suspended in limbo like a human version of St. Elmo's fire. After a brief search, Lee found a couple of old suits of foams that had been set aside in a storage bin for repair. One of them had a gaping hole under the left armpit, the other was missing its boots. Both suits were cavernous—they looked like they had been designed for sumo wrestlers.

Lee put on the suit with the armpit hole, finding that the ventilation was just about right for the above-zero nip of the bay. She spread the other out on the floor, bunching the arms as a pillow, and lay down to try to sleep.

How bizarre this whole situation was, she thought as she waited for her eyelids to gather weight. Things had seemed to gravitate so quickly from a test of professional wills into an all-out battle between good and evil. She had never believed in battles like that before. Not really. Life seemed too complex to be broken down into little pieces and then separated neatly into the white pile and the black pile. Much too complex, indeed. Yet that was how it had all come down: the good guys versus the bad guys. Here she was lying behind locked doors, under siege from the devil's own, awaiting a call on the phone that would initiate the fulfillment of heavenly prophecy.

The whole thing was very storybook.

And why her?

This wasn't the first time she had pondered that one. She'd thought about it a lot. If the Lord were going to choose a servant, it seemed like there were others around with much better qualifications. Lee had flunked out of early-morning seminary because the hour and her temperament never mixed very well back then. She liked singing in the choir, didn't care for giving talks. She studied the scriptures pretty regularly, her personal prayers had their ups and downs, and she hadn't gone much out of her way to proselyte among her co-workers, which she supposed made her something of a lukewarm missionary. Her family background was similarly run-of-the-mill. Her mother and father were fairly active. Her older brother, always exemplary, had served a mission in Syria. Her younger brother was into Nukemusic and Black Armor holograms, and his interest in church was hot and cold. But his parents had faith that he would eventually come around.

All in all, Lee suspected, she was really nothing very special. So, she asked herself, why?

And, as she thought about it, she finally came to an inescapable conclusion. She had possessed only two credentials, but they must have been the ones that had mattered. First, she had happened to show up where and when she was needed. And, second, she had said yes when she was asked. As simple as that. And now she was an inexorable part of something so vast and eternal that it was very nearly overwhelming.

On that thought she drifted off.

The noise outside the cargo doors awakened her at approximately 2:00 A.M. When her eyes first popped open she thought an avalanche was bearing down on the compound. Then her mind shook off the sleep and she realized that the compound lay in a broad valley. There were no slopes for at least a mile in either direction.

Still the sound grew, an airy rumble, like an approaching stampede.

Lee hunched her foams around her, rose to her feet and shuffled over to the doors. She pushed the vidswitch and watched the tiny screen above the temperature indicator flicker once and come on. Lee's heart froze.

A mechanical monster hovered on the screen. Its body was a fat disc, ringed with red beacons that turned the falling snow into swirling embers. Its head was a domed turret that swiveled as she watched, brandishing a thick, sawed-off tank barrel. Smaller barrels, a dozen or more, jutted at regular intervals from beneath the ring of red light. They dipped and lifted with tight precision, like stumpy, insect legs. Lee knew what they were moving for. They were taking aim.

The monster was an American hovercraft gunship, a death machine. And it was sighting in on the cargo doors.

Lee stared in disbelief. She had seen gunships before, mostly on broadcast news clips. The weapons were predominantly of U.S. origin, although many European countries employed them as part of a military arsenal. Norway, she supposed, might employ them as well. Yet in this weather, a flight from the mainland would have been absolutely unthinkable.

Then she remembered the reconnaissance station.

There was an American satellite tracking station about a mile and a half from the research compound. Hoeksberg's people maintained little contact with the military personnel there, although he had loaned them supplies on occasion when their shipments failed to come in on time. He had also given them use of the digiport pad for emergency travel. All of this philanthropy was not without direct intent, Lee knew. Hoeksberg loved having others in his debt. For months, the commanding officer at the station had owed him. Now it was undoubtedly payoff time.

The SATCOM beeped. Lee ran for it, breaking out of her shock and into swelling panic. She knocked the receiver to the floor before getting it to her ear.

The voice she heard said simply: "The end is here, Miss McKesson."

She gripped the receiver like a hand bar on a wildly pitching roller coaster.

"The very end," Hoeksberg continued with perverse sweetness, "and it is right outside your door. The end of your little escapade, the end of Mr. Roth's overrated hardware, the end of his contemptible attempts at grandstanding. The unequivocal end. Period."

"What in heavens name are you doing?" she heard herself quaver. She glanced over at the monitor again. A handful of foam-suited figures loped into position around the gunship, fire extinguishers in hand.

"Commander Gritton of U.S. Air Recon Unit Zero Thirty-Five is waiting behind the controls of a gunship just outside the cargo entrance to the digiport bay, Miss McKesson. He has learned that you are armed and dangerous, that you have become irrational, and that you have equipment at your disposal giving you the capability for limited production of miniaturized nuclear devices. I have informed him of your continued threats to digiport those devises to selected worldwide targets. I have informed him of many other things as well, but suffice it to say that, at this moment, he feels a most pressing need to remove you from your surroundings."

"You're insane!"

"You have five minutes to open the doors," Hoeksberg responded. "Just five minutes, or I will give my work, and Commander Gritton will open fire to gain entrance. Have you ever seen a DL 1250 hovercraft gunship open fire at close range, Miss McKesson?"

She swallowed. The fear tasted bitter in her mouth. She had seen pictures, yes. The projectiles were incendiary. They burned hot enough to fuse metal.

"Five minutes," he repeated, "beginning now."

Click.

She stared at the monitor. The gunship faced her, blazing red and deadly. Four figures milled around it in the driving snow, all hefting fire extinguishers in their hands. They were fellow students, no doubt. Murray, Winfield, Shelton. Maybe Greuner or Raish. All waiting for the doors to be blasted away by a rolling ball of fire, after which they would do their best to put out the flames. Perhaps they would put her out too, if there was anything left.

This was a nightmare. It was beyond belief. It was undiluted, full-strength lunacy.

It was the end.

She looked back at the equipment, lit and humming, awaiting Roth's call. Part of the plan, he had said, and he had been right. It was all part of some divinely crafted plan. Yet in five... no four and a half minutes now the entire plan was going to topple down around her ears.

Please, Lord, no. You have to do something. We've come so far, and it can't be for nothing, it just can't...

But no voice came, no angel appeared, no lightning bolt split the ceiling.

Lee's heart thumped sickly in her chest. She stepped toward the door, where the release switch to the electro-bolt stared dumbly from beside the video monitor, which glowed red with the beacons of the gunship.

Red.

Red, like the fire extinguisher that used to hang across the hall from the bay.

Of course, that fire extinguisher was gone now. It had been mangled beyond recognition, and they had replaced it months ago.

Nevertheless, it now gave Lee an idea.

She paused in mid-stride, thoughts building behind her eyes like time-lapse footage of some billowing mental thunderhead. The idea was outrageous, very nearly as insane as Hoeksberg's requisition of the gunship. Yet perhaps, for that reason, it might very well work.

She spun away from the door and scurried to the disc storage file, struggling against the foams for speed. Stripping the gloves from her hands she fumbled through the dividers, through the S's, the T's, the U's, the V's. Her breath puffed in short, cottony bursts. She stopped at the W's. The third disc in the section bore a bright red tag, along with a hand-scrawled warning:

DO NOT RUN

Above the tag was a two letter label. It read simply "WM." Which, of course, stood for "WOOLY MAMMOTH."

25

Hoeksberg slogged through the snow against the push of the wind. Up ahead, as if through a tattered curtain, the gunship waited in the blizzard. Hoeksberg was beaming wickedly. In his hand he carried a stunrifle—the same stunrifle that Winfield had torn from Lee's grasp scant hours before. In a matter of seconds, Hoeksberg was sure, he would be putting the rifle to good use. He would raise it to his shoulder, center Lee's forehead in its sights, and then he would take her down. Yes, he would take her down with relish, and then he would tie up the rest of his business in very short order.

He glanced at his chronometer. There was only a minute and a half left. He pressed alongside the gunship. The gun barrels were locked into position now. The cannon maw gleamed through a coat of clinging snow. As he watched, it telescoped slowly into firing position. The foam-suited figures stood stock still, extinguishers poised, snow shields gaping like fly-eyes in Hoeksberg's direction. He looked at his watch again.

Thirty seconds left.

The door cracked open against the snow.

Hoeksberg motioned to the gunship, and the cannon barrel sucked back into its snow coat again. The door swung wider, shoveling the loose drifts before it, spreading the crack to a foot. Two feet. Lee's bare hand came into view, pink and small at the end of a fat Thermofoam arm. Hoeksberg moved in closer, the stunrifle shouldered, the sight positioned eagerly at head-level. Any moment now, he thought. Any moment she would be his.

Then the hand pulled back and disappeared. Hoeksberg's grin clouded.

Suddenly, from the darkness inside the bay came a flutter of silent lightning. Hoeksberg stopped dead in his tracks, eyes darting, his former grin now constricting tight enough to knit his lips. He watched the light grow like a balloon, a huge, misshapen balloon of white fire. Then the fire was gone, and something dark and hulking towered in its place. Hoeksberg took a single, halting step backward.

The thing charged.

What happened next, occurred in a matter of seconds.

The mammoth burst through the doors, spraying a double fan of snow that erupted like magma in the red beams of the gunship. Hoeksberg sprawled backward, his stunrifle spinning off like a whirligig. Around him, ice crystals blew in great crimson clouds. Through the clouds, bearing down like some horrifying *deja vu*, was a pair of long ivory tusks.

Hoeksberg screamed into his foams and rolled. Past his head something pounded, something like a long-haired tree trunk powered by a pile driver. A *leg*, Hoeksberg's fevered brain screamed at him. That was just the thing's *leg!* He flailed at the drifts, struggling to right himself, and caught a glimpse of his students. They were scattering in all directions, fire extinguishers tumbling. One of the students dove under the snow and tunneled, mounding a trail like an oversized gopher. The mammoth pounded onward like a locomotive, shooting arcs of red icespray with every footfall. It had no interest in the students, none whatsoever. It was after the gunship.

The machine guns abruptly opened fire, as if suddenly breaking out of an astonishment all their own. Hoeksberg heard the bullets hit. They sounded like a volley of rocks hurled into an old rug. The mammoth didn't even slow down.

"The cannon!" Hoeksberg roared ineffectually. "Fire the cannon, you idiot!"

The mammoth bulled into the gunship with a crackling bang, tusks raking over the bright red beacons and hatching showers of sparks. Then the beast reared its head with an unearthly bellow. Trunk waving, it upended the hovercraft like a child's top. In response, the cannon finally fired. The shot was way too late. Shrieking over the roof of the compound, the projectile trailed a brilliant, blue-white tail. The recoil drove the off-balance gunship down through the snow and into the frozen earth like an oversized splitting-wedge. The machine guns now opened fire again with all the force of an impotent afterthought. Several of the barrels, crimped like drinking straws from their collision with the mammoth, bottled up the discharge and sent it blowing out of the bottom of the craft in a yellow jet. The mammoth reared back, its head and ears whipping cords of smoke. Then with a furious howl it hit the gunship again, knocking it all the way over onto its dome.

Sometime between the final machine gun blast and the mammoth's second lunge, the commander and his gunner had apparently determined discretion to be the better part of valor and had ejected themselves from the ship. Hoeksberg could see them now, scrambling away at top speed. At the same time, the vehicle's remaining beacons flashed once and died.

With something between a woof and a grunt, the mammoth backed off, shaking its head and pawing at the trampled snowpack. Then it simply turned tail and thudded off into the storm, vibrating the soles of Hoeksberg's feet like a departing earthquake.

Panting, he stood up and stared from the snowy foxhole he had unintentionally excavated. The underside of the gunship flared and spit. A second later it exploded, sending a black-orange plume rocketing into the night sky. The impact blew Hoeksberg back into his foxhole and out the other side, smearing a ten-foot trench with his person. Before the second explosion came he clambered to his feet and ran. At the last minute, out of the corner of his eye, he spied the cargo doors, wavering in the orange light.

They were neatly closed once again.

Wrath ascended inside Hoeksberg, hotter and brighter than the flames of the gunship. There would be no more talk now. The girl's chances were gone and but one course remained. One and one alone. Because Hoeksberg now no longer cared about his project. He no longer cared about the allegiance of his students, or his standing in the upper circles of the university elite. He was filled with a hellish resolve that burned away all reason, leaving only one objective scrawled on the stark, black chalkboard of his mind.

He was going to get her. He would do it all by himself if he had to, but he was going to get her and the equipment she guarded. And nothing was going to stop him.

* * *

Lee stood before the monitor screen, watching fire lick out the remains of the gunship. Miraculously, her last-ditch effort had worked. The mammoth had charged the red rim lights of the gunship, just as Lee had seen it charge the red fire extinguisher case so many months before. Moreover, the gunship had been hopelessly outmatched. Within minutes, it would be little more than smoking wreckage.

She thought about the impression that had guided her, the impression that she now knew was not of her own origination, and whispered a prayer of thanks. To it she added a prayer of godspeed for Roth. The taste of fear still lingered in her mouth. Somehow Lee sensed very strongly that she had not heard the last of Hoeksberg.

She could not have been more correct. At 3:00 A.M., with a renewed intensity that bespoke obsession, the pounding at the door began again.

26

As soon as the SATCOM receiver beeped, Roth snapped it up from amid the clutter on his desk. Hours before he had thrown caution to the wind and had contacted the Physical Sciences Department office for Miles's hotel reservation data. As it turned out, he was staying at the Regent Block in uptown San Francisco. Roth had been buzzing his vacant room long distance ever since 4:00 P.M. Finally he had left a message with the hotel desk and got the name and number of the convention center from the Regent switchboard.

By that time, things were already winding down at the convention. Roth tried to have Miles paged, but he was nowhere to be found. All of the workshops were over for the day, continuing informally throughout town in restaurants and other night spots as amiable chats between professional acquaintances. Miles now beyond his reach, Roth found no other alternative but to give up calling and wait.

Now, he prayed, the waiting would be over.

"Derek Roth's office," he blurted into the receiver.

"I have a message for a Mr. Derek Roth," the voice squawked officially. Roth recognized it as the Regent's switchboard operator.

"That's me," he said. "Shoot."

"A Mr. Daniel Miles sends his regards. He has checked out of the hotel, and is en route to the digiport terminal. He is scheduled to arrive back at his university's transport center by eleven P.M. He will call you tomorrow morning."

Eleven P.M. That was 1:00 A.M. Roth's time. Nine A.M. Lee's time.

"Thank you," Roth said breathlessly. "Thank you very much."

"You're welcome, sir," the squawk said, and clicked off.

Roth checked his chronometer. It was 12:47 A.M. He grabbed his coat and took off for the digiport center.

27

Pounding echoed through the bay.

Lee lay on the floor, bundled in foams, unable to sleep. Her nerves had reached their limit. An hour and a half ago she had started shaking and had been unable to stop. She prayed, and the shakes had finally gone away.

She was hungry and thirsty. Fortunately, she had raked a generous clump of snow inside when she had closed the cargo doors behind the mammoth. It was gritty though, and no substitute for real water. Food was even harder to come by. Lee had tried materializing a few tubers and some edible mushrooms on the pad from one of Roth's work discs, sampling each item in turn. But the mushrooms were all bitter and the tubers just gave her gas. The thought of syn-rations had never seemed so appetizing.

The wall to the left of the door was bulging now in a broad strip from top to bottom. Lee could hear several men at work out in the hall, all hammering like crazy. She didn't think there had been any more reinforcements from the recon base, though. The storm sounded too bad outside, and she doubted that a small station like that one had any more hover vehicles. Even if they had, the wind velocity might preclude their use.

The hammering went on and on.

In an effort to retain her sanity, Lee had put on the headgear to one of the thermosuits. It helped muffle some of the pounding, but not enough. So she had begun singing hymns. *A Mighty Fortress*. *Abide With Me*. *The Lord Is My Light*. *I Need Thee Every Hour*. She found after a while that the hammering formed a regular sort of rhythm that she could sing along with. The singing seemed to tame the sound somehow, nullify its threat. *How Firm A Foundation* worked best with the beat. She was singing it for the twentieth or thirtieth time when the SATCOM beeped.

"Morning babe. How you doing?" It was Roth's voice, gentle and strong.

Without the slightest warning, Lee burst into tears. She had braved Hoeksberg for days, finally fought him off at gunpoint, weathered a ten hour seige and conjured a prehistoric monster as a war machine. She had done it all without splitting a seam in her emotional fabric. But the cloth was threadbare now, and the tears just seemed to pass through it as if it were gauze. She let the tears come. They broke loose in big gasping sobs.

The slack in Roth's voice jerked instantly tight.

"What's wrong, Lee. What's happened?"

"Nothing..." she cried. That was a ludicrous statement if there ever was one. "It's okay. I'm okay. I'm just..." She let out a shaky breath between sobs. "Just tired, I guess."

"I'm at university digiport," Roth declared with reassurance. "Miles is due in any second. I think I can have the code to you in as little as twenty minutes. Can you hang in there that much longer?"

Lee squeezed her eyes shut. The walls roared around her. Twenty minutes. Twenty minutes meant thirty or forty more verses, hundreds of beats. Twenty minutes was forever.

"Yes," she said numbly. She was still crying, tears streaking her face. She was vaguely glad that Roth couldn't see her, as if that mattered. "I miss you so much."

"Oh, I miss you too," he answered with desperate longing. His voice trailed helplessly. Then it tightened with anger. "Hoeksberg's going to account for this, Lee. All of it."

"He's crazy now," she said, her own voice distant. "He called in a gunship."

"What?"

She rehearsed the whole story to him. When she got to the part about the mammoth bulldozing the hovercraft and the men scattering like ants, it all sounded unexpectedly slapstick. They both laughed a little and she felt better, the tears quenched, at least for the moment.

"How's the door holding up?" Roth asked. His voice tried to conceal its edginess. It couldn't.

"The door's doing great. The wall looks like a giant foot with a big lumpy blister on it." She sniffed. "It'll hold, though. Just hurry."

"You hang tough, babe. Twenty minutes at most, and I'll be back with the code. I love you."

He hung up.

Lee replaced her SATCOM receiver. She looked over at the wall and shuddered. She hadn't told Roth about the long crack, starting at the top of the blister and jagging its way down over the hump; the crack that gapped like a long, thin mouth, popping open and yelling "Ouch" a little louder and a little wider with every blow.

Twenty minutes, she thought. Her lip quivering, she started singing again.

28

Hoeksberg stood bare-chested, swinging the snow axe. Hair bounced on his forehead in wet curls. Sweat ran down his cheeks over clenched jaw muscles and splattered on his ribs. His eyes were stolid, unblinking. They were dull and gray, like the last ashes of some huge conflagration, ashes that were still burning hot.

Pausing for a breather, Murray watched Hoeksberg with grim fascination. Winfield and Greuner stood beside him, swinging axes of their own. Other students either sat or milled, along with Commander Gritton and his gunner, waiting for their shift to come up again. The mood was tense. Everyone knew about McKesson and the bomb threats. It was hard to believe, sure, but Murray had seen how distraught she was the moment she'd walked into the digiport bay. It had been a long eight months. She'd crashed a disc. Bugged out.

She's a good kid Murray, and you know it. Honor roll material. And she liked it here, she'd said so. So why would she go and flip off the gooney board just like that, huh? And why won't Hoeksberg even try to talk to her? And what is she supposed to be making bombs out of in there anyway? Chunks of old pottery?

Murray whupped his brain up side of the head and told it to shut up. She's bugged out, he told himself, that's all. You don't agree, you wanna argue with Hoeksberg about it?

The answer to that one was a definite NO.

Because if Hoeksberg had been acting spooky in the digiport room before all of this started, he was *really* acting spooky now. His expression hadn't changed for nearly an hour. He hadn't spoken to anyone either. He'd just stood at the door with his axe, pummeling the wall, bludgeoning it like it was something living he was trying to kill. And he didn't seem to be getting tired, that was the weirdest thing. He just kept on going, and going and going, like...

Like a man possessed.

Winfield mopped his brow and shoved a snow axe into Murray's hand for his next shift. Murray held up the blade and looked at it. It was dulled to nearly nothing. The two men glanced at each other, and the look that passed between them acknowledged the incredible craziness of the whole situation. How could this go on? How could it possibly go on?

Then Murray's gaze slipped past Winfield to Hoeksberg, whose burning, ashen eyes told him to take his turn and take it now.

Right now.

Murray stepped into position and started swinging.

29

Dan Miles stood outside the door of his lab, tapping at the security keypad next to his office door. But he wasn't really watching what he was doing. He was talking to Roth.

"He's a good kid, Derek. Real good kid," Miles beamed, expounding on the extremely lengthy accomplishments of his only son. "Starts at Dartmouth next semester, did I tell you?"

Roth smiled, nodded, and took a furtive glance at his chronometer. "Yeah, you did. Wish I could meet him." He shuffled nervously, doing his best to remain casual. He had met Miles just as he had stepped off the main pad at the university center. He was obviously tired, but his face had brightened at the sight of an old acquaintance. They had exchanged greetings, Roth explaining that he was working on a special project and needed to borrow something from Miles' lab. Miles was headed for his office anyway, and the two had headed off together.

It took them fifteen minutes to cover the hundred yards or so between the digiport center and the Physical Sciences Building. It had been months since the two men had seen each other, and Roth had forgotten that Miles was such a talker. Out of sheer courtesy, he felt obliged to engage in some visiting. After all they had scarcely spoken for two semesters, and Roth was here to ask a favor. But under the circumstances, renewing old times had its limit, and Roth found himself getting progressively edgy. The twenty-minute deadline he had mentioned to Lee was a minute and a half past already.

"He's majoring in cybernetics," Miles went on. "Real whiz. They gave him a full ride, plus fees and priority housing." He punched the enter key, and an ERROR signal came up on the LED for the second time. Miles was obviously more interested in his conversation than he was in getting his storeroom unlocked. "He'll be home for the holidays. We'll have to have you over for dinner. Anna waves up a mean syn-turkey, dressing and the whole bit."

"Sounds great," Roth said. He shifted to his other foot as Miles started in on the keyboard again. Three times Roth had almost come out and told him everything, just to put a fire under his tail. Three times he had closed his mouth again, wiped his palms on his pants and kept fidgeting. Because there was really no way to tell him. Was there?

Get a move on, would you Dan? You see, I have this graduate student whom I've fallen in love with, and she's waiting about five thousand miles from here with some newfangled electronic equipment I invented. It's gonna help us bring back the Lost Ten Tribes of Israel. You know, from the lands of the North. Only problem is, her faculty advisor is in league with the devil. And he's gone bonkers, and right now he's trying to beat down the walls so he can get in and get at her. We're both a little jumpy about the whole thing, and so I'd really appreciate it if you'd GET THE LEAD OUT AND MOVE!"

"You nervous?" Dan asked him suddenly. "You look kind of nervous." His fingers were skipping over the keys for the third time, no more carefully than they had the other two times. Roth looked at them.

"In kind of a hurry, that's all. Have to finish this project up tonight."

"Real cruncher, huh?"

"Definitely."

As Miles eyed him the lock finally gave in, clacking dully inside the wall. The door swung open and the lights inside came on automatically.

"What is it you need, anyway? Hope it's not one of those little field force converters everybody borrows. We got rid of those last semester and installed heavy duty—"

Roth cut him off as politely as he could.

"Just need a spectrograph, Dan. You still keep them all on microdisc, don't you?" Spectrographs were way out of his everyday realm, but he still remembered them from Physics 202. Every element gave off a distinct color when it burned. A spectrograph was like a picture of those colors, which were displayed as bands on a linear scale. Astronomers like Miles used spectrographs to analyze the chemical composition of individual stars. For convenience in storage, the readings were usually translated into electronic data and stored on disc.

"Oh, yeah," Miles said, moving to the storeroom door. He punched another set of keys, and this time the door opened on the first try. "Got 'em all on disc. One of the biggest collections in the country. Nearly every star visible from our position in the galaxy. And a few more besides. What kind of project you doing with spectrographs anyway?"

"If it works," Roth said, "I'll tell you all about it."
And it had better, his brain echoed.

Dan grunted, slid open a wall compartment just inside the door and turned a key. The drawers unlocked with a buzz and a click. He turned to Roth.

"How many you need?"

"Just one," Roth said. He felt the tingling of goosebumps on his lower arms.

"I need Polaris. The North Star."

Three minutes later Roth emerged from the building with a disc in his hand. He headed toward his office where a satellite communicator and a minicomputer, complete with modem, sat on the corner of his desk. After a second, he broke into a trot. Then a run.

He had the key to the Millennium File.

30

Lee had stopped singing. She just sat in the chair in front of the scanner keyboard, the SATCOM in her lap. Her face was drawn, her eyes dark and ringed. Her muscles twitched each time the wall took an exceptionally loud blow.

She was tired, and thirsty, and hungry, and very afraid.

The crack was yawning now, gaping and roaring like the mouth of a toothless lion with every report.

She tried not to think about it. She tried to think about Roth, and the code that was going to come in over the SATCOM any second. Yes, the code would come soon, and she would send it through to the computer, and the computer would send the data to the pad. And then, behold and lo, the armies of ancient Israel would pour onto the pad in a phalanx of light. And along with them would come their women and children, thousands of them, streaming into the room and bursting the walls; a solid mass of humanity, mowing Hoeksberg down like a reed in a typhoon. Lee pictured it. And she embraced it, because she didn't want to consider the alternative.

The other vision, which kept knocking at the back door of her mind, was the one of Hoeksberg breaking down the door, getting into the bay before Roth ever sent the code.

I'm going to hurt you, Miss McKesson. I'm going to hurt you very, very badly...

The image of his face still haunted her, that leering, yellow face, bobbing like some devilish apparition.

And that was four days ago, her mind kept crying out, *four whole days ago. That was back when things were still reasonably normal and sensible and sane. What has he become by now?*

There was a sudden rush of sound from behind the ravaged wall. It wrenched Lee from her grim reverie.

BANG!

She started violently, nearly losing her balance. The blade of a snow axe punched brutally through the crack in the wall, just under the middle door hinge. It wriggled out and punched again. The wall crackled and rocked. The hinge rattled, loosening.

Lee screamed into her hands.

The SATCOM beeped. She grabbed it.

"I've got it, Lee. You ready?"

Roth's voice was crisp and tight over the line. It sounded beautiful. A chorus of angels could never have sounded better, she was sure of it.

"Yeah, I'm ready!" Lee gasped. Then she remembered the tiny door to the digiport maintenance compartment. It was open, effectively blocking any incoming signals. Including the signals from the scanner gear.

"No! Wait..!" She dropped the SATCOM and leaped behind the console, groping for the opening. She found the door and jammed it shut. The MAINTENANCE signal left the countdown window.

BANG!

The middle hinge fell away, and two more pick blades pierced the wall.

Lee snatched up the SATCOM again.

"Okay, I'm ready!" She was breathless. The words were no more than gasps. "But hurry please hurry, he's coming *through the wall!*"

BANG! BANG!

The bottom hinge drooped like a tired salute.

Lee squirmed against the panic, but it had her, like a monstrous fist it had her and it was squeezing. *"What's the sequence? Tell me what to do?"*

"Stay calm," Roth's voice said. It cracked. "I'm all set on this end. It just takes three keystrokes on yours. Hit M first."

She punched the key, and the bottom hinge popped off the wall with an earsplitting crack. The lower corner of the door jerked inward, gapping.

"Yeah, M!" she yelled into the receiver. "Next!"

"Space bar."

What sounded like an army of axe blades suddenly attacked the top hinge in a vicious barrage. Lee pounded the space bar.

"Next!"

"Function 12. Then lay the receiver on the modem. I'll send!"

The hinge groaned, coughing out a bolt. It clattered to the floor amid the pounding, the cracking, the smashing. Lee scanned the keyboard frantically, her words tumbling out in sheer terror.

"Where's function 12? I can't find it! Where is it?"

She knew where Function 12 was. She had used it before, hadn't she? Only now it was gone. It had disappeared. It had ceased to exist. And behind her, the hinge was giving way, and the door was going to fall in any second she could hear it.

"Top! Just left of center!"

She found it and punched, reeling with premature relief.

"The receiver Lee! Put the receiver on the..!"

She slammed it onto the modem. The screen beeped and came alive with symbols.

Behind her there was a coarse ripping sound. She spun and looked. The last hinge was tearing loose, taking a three-foot section of wall with it.

The screen beeped again and went blank. Lee's hand, shaking like mad, fluttered across the keyboard. And just as it found the SEND key, the door fell inward, twisting on the latch and thundering to the floor.

There was a scream, like the howl of a crazed animal. Hoeksberg raced in over the door, axe in hand. Lee saw him only for the briefest instant, but in that split second she felt a rush of complete terror, a ghastly confirmation that all of her tortured imaginings had been real.

He wasn't coming for the equipment. He was coming for her.

Lee's finger jerked downward.

SEND!

And the entire pad erupted like a solar flare. Hoeksberg screamed again, dropping the axe and shielding his face, like a vampire cringing before the sun. Then he stumbled and fell, his entire body washing out white in the glare. The light danced crazily, then locked into place, then began to congeal.

Lee covered her eyes, stepping back into the computer and knocking the SATCOM receiver from the modem to the floor. All of her terror was suddenly gone, wiped away like a frost before the rays of dawn. Now she felt joyous, exultant, incredibly fulfilled. And in spite of the intense radiance on the pad, she lowered her hand from her face and looked.

* * *

Sitting helplessly in his office, Roth lifted his own receiver from his modem and listened. At first all he could hear was the buzz of the pad, a hoarse scream, the thud of something falling to the floor. Then there was another sound, small at first, but rising steadily and finally swelling to the point that he had to pull the SATCOM from his ear.

It was the babble of an enormous crowd.

Non-English babble.

They had done it. It was finished.

Roth just listened for a minute, his face empty, his eyes blank with disbelief. Then he started to laugh. He leaned back in his chair in complete and unrestrained ecstasy and tossed the receiver into the air with a jubilant whoop of victory.

Outside his window, across the quad, a handful of students heard him. They glanced up for just a second before continuing on their way, perhaps wondering, only in passing, what all the commotion was about. Like the rest of the world, they would learn soon enough.